holdin' on

The H Books #2.5

TRACY BROEMMER

Holdin' On

The H Books, Book 2.5

by

Tracy Broemmer

Contemporary Romance Novella

Published by Tracy Broemmer

Edited by Lexie Broemmer

Cover by Designed with Grace

All Rights Reserved

ISBN#: 978-1-951637-27-9

1

"**D**id you sleep with him?"

Journey Ryan froze in the act of pulling her black hair up off her neck. Felt like Dalton had the heat up to crackling, and she had already shed her coat and hoodie. She glanced at him now, a little bit stunned by his question. Surely, she'd heard him wrong.

"What?" Slowly, she tugged her ponytail through the elastic band and lowered her hands to stare at her little brother's friend. To his credit, Dalton kept his eye on the road ahead of them, his right hand relaxed on the wheel.

"Abbott." He glanced at her. "Isn't that his name? That guy you were with at your dad's party?"

Journey fidgeted with the oversized silver band she wore on her right middle finger as she considered how to answer him. Dalton McKenzie used to be a staple in her house, like a second little brother. Back in those days, Journey had mostly thought of him as another pain in her ass, yet another kid for her parents to like better than her.

At least someone to keep her brother, Kendric, busy most of the time.

Dalton had left town for school. Before her father's party, she hadn't seen him in years—at least five. She had no idea how to take his question. True, she had talked to him for a while at the party. She'd even danced with him a few times. But even that had been over a month ago.

"What?" she said again.

When he reached to turn the radio down, Journey's eyes followed his hand, but she locked eyes with him again when he lifted his gaze to hers.

"What're you doing?"

"I dunno." He shrugged. "Can you not hear me? Did you sleep with Bryant Abbot?"

Journey leaned sideways and turned the radio up. She didn't love Dalton's music choice, at least not today. For Pete's sake, they were on the way to Kristophe House for a Christmas getaway. It was the second weekend in December. Was it too much to ask to hear some holiday music? When she had said that to Dalton earlier, he'd narrowed his eyes at her and stared at her like she had morphed into a short green alien.

"Really?" He tipped his head at her and rolled his eyes. "An hour ago, you were griping about Aerosmith."

"I wasn't griping about Aerosmith," she corrected him. She liked Aerosmith. Particularly "Janie's Got a Gun." But hello? December? Fun trip? Festive music? "I just asked if we could listen to Christmas music."

"Tell ya what."

She didn't like the sound of that. Rather than watch Dalton drive—the guy was huge, big surprise he'd played Division I football in school—she turned to look out the windshield at the snowflakes that swirled in a whirlpool pattern in the beams of his SUV's headlights.

"I'll give you full control of the music."

Looked like it was coming down harder now. Faster. Thicker. Something. She wasn't particularly worried about getting to the bed and breakfast. She was worried, however, about the rest of the gang. They'd all agreed on a later start, since everyone was working at least until five.

"If you tell me if you slept with him."

At this rate, Journey was kind of sorry she hadn't just waited. She could have caught a ride with Vanessa and Parker. For some reason—most likely temporary insanity —she had been all in when Dalton suggested they head on up and get the lay of the land.

"I saw Aerosmith in concert once," she told him, eyes still straight ahead. "Did I tell you that?"

"No."

She wondered if he would let it go now. She hadn't slept with Bryant Abbott. Ever. And it wasn't that big of a deal, but she wasn't sure why Dalton needed to know. They were friends years ago, sure, but they had never been the kinds of friends to share popsicles or secrets. More like Journey snorted and made fun of Dalton and her brother for their celebrity crushes and Dalton and Kendric made snide comments as she left the house to go out on dates.

"Dric said you didn't date him for very long."

She huffed out a sigh. Nope. Apparently, Dalton wasn't going to let it go.

"I didn't date him."

"But he was your date for the party."

"Lenore threw a ridiculously extravagant party for my

father. And she instructed me to bring a date. Bryant and I know each other through work. We're friends."

Well. Sort of. Maybe not so much. After the party. When Bryant thought they were going to take things to the next level. Again, Journey didn't really want to discuss it with Dalton. In fact, she had talked—vented—to Vanessa and Mercedes, another friend, and it happened over a month ago, so there was no point in digging it back up.

"You danced with him."

Journey turned to look at Dalton. "Danced with you, too. But I didn't sleep with you."

"So, you did sleep with him."

"Why?" She rested her head on the seat behind her and closed her eyes. "Why does it matter?"

"I was gone for several years, Journey. Just trying to get caught up on things."

"Why don't you wanna catch up on my job? Or on who Dric's dating now, or if I still like skiing, or if I prefer crunchy peanut butter to smooth?"

"Speaking of jobs." He tapped his fingers to the rhythm on the wheel and glanced at her again. "I heard your dad's talking about retiring."

She nodded. "Yeah. It's a little early, but I think he and Lenore are going to do some traveling."

"Why do you call her Lenore? Kendric doesn't."

"Kendric is her favorite child. Lenore and I tolerate each other."

"Bullshit."

Journey rolled her head his way on the seat and blinked her eyes open.

"It's complicated," she said quietly.

"You look like her."

"Biology." Journey cleared her throat. "Lots of nature. Not a lot of nurture."

"She still smoke weed?"

"Yep."

"More nature, huh?"

Journey snorted and shook her head. "Yeah, I guess so." Back to the snowflakes. Fatter and thicker, still.

"So, did you?"

"No. I *did not* sleep with Bryant Abbott the night of my dad's party. Nor have I ever in my life slept with Bryant Abbott, nor do I have any desire to sleep with him. Ever."

Dalton was silent in the wake of her outburst.

Expecting him to—well, hell, if she knew, but she'd expected SOME kind of response after he'd asked the question several times—she finally turned to look at him again. Inside the SUV, his sparse, buzz cut hair looked dark, but she knew in real daylight, it was a nice honey blonde. The kind women paid her best friend Vanessa to do for them.

Dalton finally nodded, thoughtfully, as if he was going over lines in a play.

"Hmm."

Journey flinched as if he had slapped her.

"Wait." She tipped her head to study him closely. "That's it? That's all you have to say?"

Dalton shrugged. He opened his mouth to answer her, but Journey cut him off.

"No, no, no. No. Wait. You didn't even *say* anything. You *harrumphed* me. What the hell, Dalton? That sounded like something my grandfather would do."

"I asked, you answered."

He sounded so damned nonchalant; Journey's fingers twitched with the need to slap him.

"But."

Irritated now, ready to dig into this conversation, Journey unbuckled her seatbelt, scooched around to sit sideways, and glanced out the windshield once more as she reached blindly to click the buckle again.

"It's getting slick."

Journey eyed him silently for a moment. What guy admitted to slick roads when he was driving? None she knew. The men in her life—brother, father, losers she'd dated—all acted like they were smarter than the weather and women, too, and could handle driving blindfolded with a hand tied behind their backs through a hurricane of snow and farm animals blowing around them.

"How much farther do we have to go?"

She still wasn't worried about getting to Kristophe House. Now, she was worried that she might be stuck overnight with just Dalton if the rest of the gang waited until tomorrow to get on the road.

"Mmm." Dalton pursed his lips in thought.

She watched his eyes move to the clock radio and back to the road. It was just after five, but darkness had slammed them pretty quickly once they got on the road. Her feet were hot now. Dear God, was this big brute of a guy coldblooded?

"Maybe an hour?" He kind of wiggled his lips a bit.

Journey leaned sideways to tug her Uggs off.

"Jesus, Journey, what's next? Your jeans? Or your T-shirt?"

"Why do you have the heat on full blast?" she griped. "It's hotter than the surface of the sun in here."

"I thought you were cold."

She laughed softly when he reached to turn the heat down.

"Thank you." She wiggled her toes, relieved to get the boots off.

"Hmm."

"What?"

"Maybe you should take off your shirt or your jeans."

"What?"

"Do you wear underwear?"

"What?" She shook her head. "Dalton, did you have one too many head injuries in football? What the hell are you talking about?"

"Your feet are bare in your shoes. Just sayin'..."

Realization dawning on her, she cut loose with a hearty laugh. "You wish."

"Maybe." He grinned.

His playlist started over. Journey barely held in a groan as she leaned forward to snap the power button off.

"What're you doing?"

"Only so many times I can hear 'Dude Looks Like a Lady." She stared at him boldly, daring him to argue. "Besides, I answered your question, so I should get to choose what we listen to now."

"Just know that if you put Bing on my radio, I'm not responsible for what might happen."

"Do you mean that in a good way or bad? Like are you pro-Bing or not?"

"Not."

"Interesting." She turned the radio on and tapped through the XM stations until she recognized Ella Fitzgerald singing "Sleigh Ride."

"Why is that interesting?"

"How can you not like Bing?"

"I don't love Bing," he answered with an exaggerated shrug. "Why didn't you sleep with Bryant Abbott?"

"That's hardly the same thing. It's not even a relevant question. It doesn't make sense."

"Just answer me."

"Dalton—" Journey sighed and rubbed her eyes. "I never thought I'd say this, but I miss the pain-in-the-ass twelve-year-old version of you."

"Not true." He shook his head. "We had fun at your dad's party. And we had fun a lot of nights when I was home during college."

Point, Dalton. They weren't close, but Journey and her brother were. So, yes, she saw Dalton when he was home from school, and they partied together, with at least 50 other people around.

"His lips were too red."

Again, her comment was met with silence from Dalton. Ella Fitzgerald's voice segued into Elton John singing "Step Into Christmas."

"What?"

When Dalton did finally turn to look at her, the amused look on his face made her wish she could take it back. Why had she opened her mouth?

"You heard me," she mumbled as she turned her face away from him. If he was going to laugh about that, he would really tease her for blushing now.

"His lips," Dalton started. "Right? His lips? His lips were too red?"

"Yep."

"Journey, what does that even mean?"

"I just don't like it."

"But I mean. How? How are a guy's lips too red? Like lipstick red?"

"Some guys are just kind of pale. Almost vampiric. And they're sort of…posh-looking. Soft. And because of that, their lips look too red."

Journey didn't look at him this time. She was content to ride the rest of the way to Kristophe House in silence. A gross, uncomfortable silence, but still.

"There's just so much there, I don't know where to start."

His comment came out of left field at least ten minutes later. Three songs had played and changed between her announcement and his comment.

"Let's just not." She turned to him and offered him a sweet smile.

"So. Okay, first. Posh-looking. What? What is that? What does that mean?"

Journey jumped when her phone rang. Dalton gave her a look when her holiday ringtone blared in his SUV.

"Seriously? You don't strike me as such a festive person."

"What does that mean?"

She was curious what he meant, but when she pulled her phone from her purse, she looked down at the screen to find that Vanessa Mayne was calling her.

2

———

She looked anxious as she raised her phone to her ear. Dalton glanced at her, but the weather was getting dicey. He wasn't worried about getting to the bed and breakfast safely, but the roads were a bit slick. Best to pay attention, even if he would rather look at Kendric Ryan's sister.

"Hey." Journey spoke quietly into her phone. "What's up?"

He wondered who was calling her. Most likely one of their friends who was supposed to meet them for the weekend. If it were Kendric, would he call her or Dalton? Then again, if it was Kendric calling, Dalton figured she would have put him on speaker phone.

The Christmas music didn't really bother him. He had argued with her earlier for the sake of arguing. Journey Ryan had always been such an easy target. She hid it well. Always had. But Dalton had always known when he got under her skin.

Take now, for instance.

Asking her about Bryant Abbott. True, he wanted to know, but the fact that his ribbing her about Abbott bugged her made him happy. He wasn't sure why he liked to torment her—well, okay, he was attracted to her. Always had been. But he knew better. Kendric would probably rip his balls off and slam them down his own throat if he knew some of the thoughts he'd had about Journey.

Besides, Dalton McKenzie was never the guy the pretty girls picked. Put him next to a guy like Bryant Abbott, and the girls picked Abbott and then proceeded to buddy up to Dalton to work an introduction or a meet-cute. Yep, he actually had women admit that to him now. He was the good guy. The funny guy. The joker. The buddy. And women told him that because he was good-natured about it and let it roll off his back.

When Journey ended the call and rested her cheek on the seat, Dalton eyed her curiously. She sighed and tipped her head up to look at him.

"Van and Parker are gonna wait and head up in the morning."

Vanessa Mayne had been Journey's best friend since the beginning of time. Dalton had enjoyed messing with her, too, but Vanessa blew him off in a way Journey couldn't manage. If he wasn't a smart guy, that might make him wonder. Good thing he knew Journey was out of his league.

"Yeah, if it's coming down like this back home, I don't blame them," he agreed, shooting another searching look out the driver's window.

"You sure we should keep going?"

"Well, we're a lot closer to Kristophe House now than

we are home." He shrugged. "It's not that bad yet, but I think we're better off just going as planned. No telling what we would find on the roads on the way home."

She nodded and looked back at the road.

"Tell me again what you do."

"I'm an R.N. I was working in an ED in Texas," he told her.

"Did you like it?"

"I did." He tapped his fingers again on the steering wheel.

"Then why'd you come home?'

"My dad's not in good health." He didn't want to talk about it, so he attempted to head off any further questions. "My mom didn't ask me to come home, but it felt important to be here."

"I understand." Journey's voice was soft and compassionate. "What will you do now?"

"I have three interviews next week when we get back home." Dalton glanced at her, pleased to find her big violet eyes on him, clearly interested in what he had to say. "One at the psych ward. And one in ICU. And then one for the head of nursing at Innsbruck Memory Care."

"Oh wow." She flinched a bit, but Dalton read concern in her eyes, rather than impatience or disgust. "They all sound really heavy."

"It's what I do." He blew off her concern, because that's what he always did when a woman out of his league showed him any.

"Have you always been in emergency medicine?" she asked him.

"Yeah, started there fresh out of school. It's a good fit."

Dalton was a big guy. Mostly muscle, although since

he'd been out of school and away from football, some of his bulk had gotten soft. He figured it was another reason —if not the main one—why women would always choose a pretty boy like Bryant Abbot over him. Still, his bulk made him good for emergency situations that involved drug abusers or violent patients, whether their intent was to harm others or themselves.

"Yeah." She offered him a small, honest smile. "It is. I'm sure you're an excellent nurse, Dalton."

He didn't hear sarcasm in her voice, and he heard it often enough that he should recognize it if it was there. But still, praise made him as uncomfortable as concern, so he deflected again.

"So. Back to Abbott's ruby red lips."

Journey groaned.

"Why? Why do we have to go back to that? I've spent more time on him right now than ever before."

"Dric said you guys dated for a while."

"We didn't. And why is Dric talking to you about who I date?"

"He doesn't usually. But he hates that guy."

"Bryant?"

"Yeah."

"Hmm." She frowned but shook her head.

"What do you mean by soft? Posh-looking?"

"Silver spoons. No manual labor ever. Bryant was okay, but his face, all around his lips, his face looked drained of color. And then there were his ruby red lips."

"And that's a turn off for you?"

"Yes."

"Hmm."

"Nope. If you get to badger me about what I like and don't like about men, I get more than a *hmm* in response."

"I'm not badgering you about men. Just asking about Abbott."

"You're badgering me."

"I just find it interesting." Dalton tossed his hand up and then just as quickly wrapped his fingers around the wheel again.

"I think the exit is up here just a few miles," she told him just as the GPS on his phone announced the same thing. "Why is it interesting?"

"Most women swoon over guys like that."

Journey sat quietly, apparently considering his comment. Finally, she arched her eyebrows and shook her head.

"I'm not most women, Dalton. You know that."

He did know that. He had always known that. Journey was tough, a little bit blunt, but fiercely loyal. Dalton knew for a fact that she would do anything for her brother; she had bailed him out of trouble many times when they were younger. Including the handful of times she literally bailed him out of jail for underage drinking. He also knew that their mother did tend to favor Kendric, though Dalton knew Dric hated the distance between Lenore and Journey.

Probably why Journey was so independent, which was probably a good thing. The woman could change a flat tire, change the oil in her car, fix most household appliance problems, and calculate most math problems in her head. She was tiny compared to Dalton, but he'd known better back in their younger days, to think that meant she was physically weak. Journey had played basketball in school; Dalton had watched her play a lot, just because he had always been around her brother and her family. Because she was smaller, she was a guard. Because she had dazzling ball handling skills, she was point guard as a freshman.

Dalton assumed she was still as bossy and tough today as she was fifteen years ago.

"Do you like your job?"

She managed a parcel delivery service that Dalton knew did a decent business. It also meant she probably worked with a lot of men, and even if she managed the office, she probably still did some heavy lifting. He could take her in arm-wrestling—with the pinky of his non-dominant hand— but he wouldn't doubt that she could take Kendric down.

When she didn't answer, Dalton looked over at her. She lifted her hand to signal that he should take the exit. He did without comment.

"I do. And I don't." She tipped her head. "It's fine. Just. Boring sometimes."

"When you got your business degree, what did you want to do with it?"

"I don't know," she hedged. "I don't think I wanted to do anything specific with it. I just wanted to make sure I had a degree. I didn't want to be like Lenore. I didn't want to drift. So, I chose business. I mean, it wasn't any more passionate than if I had thrown a dart at a poster in a guidance counselor's office and chosen a career field that way."

Dalton glanced at her again. She sounded a little defeated.

"So, instead of drifting like Lenore...instead of trying a

little of this and a little of that, I got a degree and worked merchandising at a warehouse for a few years. And then got on where I'm at. Worked my way up. So, I drift in and out in my workplace."

He hated that he had dragged her down, though he wasn't sure he could say he killed a party. She was frustrated with him for badgering her about her date for her dad's party, so he wasn't sure which was the better topic to pursue now.

"In hindsight, maybe I didn't do much better than Lenore."

"She was pregnant at seventeen."

Dalton cringed. He probably shouldn't have said that. For one thing, it wasn't his business. Sure, he and Kendric had discussed it often. And Journey had been in on the conversation a time or two, thrown out some opinions after having too much to drink. But it was a sore spot. For Lenore. For Journey.

"Okay, so I managed not to do that," she mumbled.

"Do you want kids? A family?"

He slowed the SUV at Kristophe Lane and made a left. They would arrive within fifteen minutes, but it wasn't soon enough for Dalton. His stomach was growling; he hadn't eaten since his early lunch at eleven.

"I don't know." Journey sounded surprised that she didn't know how to answer him. "I thought I did."

"But now you don't?"

"I don't know. I mean…I don't want kids before—if I do the family thing, I want to do it in the right order."

That didn't surprise him. Lenore and Sherwin hadn't gotten married until Journey was five and Lenore found out she was pregnant with Kendric.

"Nothing wrong with that."

"Well, I mean." She tipped her head at him and narrowed her eyes. "It's what I want. I'm not saying it's not okay for other people."

Dalton stole another peek at her. Chin tipped down now, she studied her hands. Vulnerability wasn't a look she wore often; Dalton had only seen it once or twice. He doubted she would appreciate his instinct to slide closer and put his arm around her.

"What about you?" She cleared her throat and looked at him, eyes wide with curiosity.

"Do I want a family?"

She nodded.

"I do."

But. He didn't say more. No way was he going to get into the fact that none of the relationships he had ever been in had been real. That he'd thought so, but no woman had ever seriously entertained the idea of falling in love with him.

"Yeah?" Journey quirked an eyebrow at him. "Got someone special in Texas waiting for you to settle in so she can join you?"

"No."

Dalton was happy to see the warm porch light glowing off to the west of the lane. Pulling up at the bed and breakfast and having to speak to the hosts was the perfect way to kill this conversation. Maybe he and Journey would find something to fix for dinner together, shoot the breeze for a while, and then part company for the night. Dalton had heard her talking to Vanessa about packing some books to read. And Dalton was ready to kick back and binge some TV.

No more conversation about feelings or relationships. Kendric would either show up later with Erin, or they would arrive tomorrow when Journey's friends did. Either way, the catching up between him and Journey had officially ended.

3

Sylvia, the hostess at Kristophe, hovered longer than Journey thought was necessary. While she appreciated the woman's hospitality, Journey was concerned about the woman's trek over possibly dangerous roads to get back to wherever home was. The woman showed Journey and Dalton around the rambling old farmhouse fixed up to be surprisingly charming and then showed them where to find extra blankets if needed, towels for the shower, and other items like the snow shovel and salt.

She insisted on dishing up bowls of homemade vegetable soup for them. Plated warm biscuits straight from the oven. Promised them Joel—Journey assumed he was her husband—would be by in the morning to clear the drive for them with the snowblade, assured them her vehicle was indeed four-wheel drive and she could handle the short drive to her home just a few miles on down the road, and finally headed out.

After the woman's bubbly, talkative exploration of the

house, Journey found the silence in the big, old kitchen almost unbearable. Sitting across the butcher block table from Dalton, after the conversation on the drive here, she had no idea what to say to him.

"Do you want a beer?"

She jumped at his question, his voice almost echoing in the cavernous room. Journey looked around at the white country cabinets and wondered where he had seen beer. Sylvia had welcomed them to anything in the kitchen, and she hadn't specifically said no alcohol. But Journey hadn't noticed any in the refrigerator, either.

"There's beer?" She tipped her head, spoon in hand. The soup was thick and steaming hot, and she couldn't wait to take a bite.

"Cooler in the SUV."

"You brought a cooler of beer?" She grinned.

"Yes."

"I knew you were good for something," she said with a soft laugh. "Yes, please."

Dalton walked away with a small smile on his face. Inside the house, in the glow of the kitchen lights, his hair was that honey blonde she remembered. He had always worn it short, even when Kendric had grown his out for a man bun for a year or so. Now Dalton had thinning hair on top and the rest cut in a military buzz. His warm smile and his bulk kind of gave him a big teddy bear look. Far cry from that skinny tween he had been when he started hanging out with Kendric.

Journey hated that Vanessa and Parker weren't going to make it tonight. But she understood. If the roads were getting slick and the snow was coming down harder back home, she wouldn't want them on the road anyway. Add in the fact that Vanessa was carrying precious cargo—Journey was betting on a baby girl—they had absolutely made the right decision.

She dipped into the soup and savored the thick, bold taste before swallowing. Though she loved food, she hated cooking and rarely did since she lived alone. Vanessa didn't cook often, but Journey loved it when her friend invited her over for a meal. Even better were the few times Mercedes and Nick—Parker's brother—had invited her over for dinner at their house. Mercedes claimed to be nothing special, but Journey figured the woman could make bread and water delicious.

"Still coming down out there."

Journey looked up to watch Dalton lug the heavy cooler in through the back door. Her eyes roamed over his broad shoulders, noting the slide of muscle under his gray thermal T-shirt. Snowflakes clung to his shoulders and sleeves; when he finally turned to her to offer her a longneck, Journey noticed his eyelashes were wet and clumpy.

"Is it still just snow?"

"Kind of a mix. Little bit of freezing rain."

"Great." She tried to suppress a sigh. Would the rest of their gang even be able to make it tomorrow if the winter weather continued? "Thanks." She took the beer as he sat down, but she couldn't drag her eyes from his face. His cheeks were ruddy from the cold, and his pale lips looked a bit dry and chapped.

"What?" Dalton tipped his head at her. "What's—?" He looked down at himself as if checking for a spill.

"Nothing." Journey finally stirred and shook her head. "Weren't you cold out there?"

"I'm hotter than hell after that drive up here," he answered as he twisted the top off his bottle. "I assumed like most females you're coldblooded and would want the heat on a gazillion."

She snorted and opened her bottle. "Thank you, Dalton." Her smile was sincere. "I'm not like most females. In fact, I don't think I'm like many females at all."

"I don't, either." He shrugged. "But I was trying to be nice."

"That was very nice of you," she agreed. "Look at it this way. We drove up here in a sauna, so now we're good to down a few beers."

"I like how you think."

Journey turned her attention back to the bowl in front of her. "Most guys don't."

"How's the soup?" he asked, evidently choosing to ignore her mumble.

"Really good."

He caught her eye when she looked up. Journey held the eye contact for a second and then looked away.

"So." She cleared her throat. "Your dad."

"Cancer." She couldn't miss the edge in his voice. "Pancreatic cancer."

"Oh God, Dalton." She flinched. "I'm sorry."

He gave her a curt nod, but when he didn't seem inclined to say more, Journey scrambled for something else to say.

"So, what about your brother?" Dalton beat her to it.

"What about Dric?"

"Is he pretty serious about Erin?"

"How would I know?"

"He says you guys talk a lot."

Again, Journey wondered why Kendric and Dalton would ever talk about her. She studied Dalton's face for a moment before looking at her bottle.

"We do. But he doesn't say a lot about Erin." She took a drink. "Talk about his job a lot."

"You know about Keely, right?"

Journey nodded and held her breath. How could not know about the one woman who had broken her brother?

"I think he's been afraid to trust anyone again," she mumbled. "And it feels weird to talk about him with you."

Dalton nodded.

"We're crossing items off the acceptable-things-to-talk-about list in record time. Pretty soon we'll be condemned to silence."

At his words, Journey jerked her chin back up to stare at him boldly. He was right. They were going to end up wasting a perfect night in uncomfortable silence. But she wasn't sure what to do about it. She hadn't seen Dalton enough since they were kids to feel close to him, and Journey didn't trust easily, anyway.

"I brought books," she said with a smirk.

"And reading a book would be preferable to talking to me?"

"You just said we're gonna be condemned to silence."

"What can we talk about? You said no red lips. No sex. I don't particularly want to discuss my dad. You don't wanna talk about Dric. Or your mother."

"Lenore is never a good topic." She rested her spoon in her bowl and rubbed her eyes.

"What're you reading?"

"What?"

Dalton spooned the last of his soup and shrugged. Journey stared at his empty bowl in stunned silence. She still had more than half a bowl left.

"Tell me what you're reading."

"*Watership Down.*"

"What?"

"It's a classic—"

"I know what it is." Dalton rolled his eyes. "But. Why?"

"Why not?"

"I figured you'd be reading the latest Sylvia Day book or something."

"You know who Sylvia Day is?"

"I work with a lot of women. And we..." He arched his eyebrows and puckered his lips and finally gave into the laugh. "We all share books. So, while I haven't read any Sylvia Day books, I know who she is."

"I don't care much for romance," Journey said simply.

"Books?"

Books or otherwise, but Journey didn't care to jump into that conversation, either, so she answered with a noncommittal nod and shrug.

"Okay, so, we talked about books." Dalton pushed his bowl away and looped his fingers loosely around the neck of his bottle. "Last movie you saw."

"I watch movies all the time."

"At the theater?"

"No. Haven't done that in...I don't even know how long. Maybe *Magic Mike*?"

"That was like fifteen years ago!" he yelped in surprise.

"No, it wasn't, but it has been a long time."

"So, you're into Channing Tatum."

"Um. Yeah." She nodded and rolled her eyes. "Who isn't?"

"Which means, his lips aren't too red for your liking."

Journey laughed softly and shook her head. "You're never gonna let that go, are you?"

"I'm just…intrigued. I wanna know what you mean."

"Adam Yarrow."

Dalton shook his head. "Who?"

"Don't you watch TV?"

"Sports." Dalton shrugged.

Journey groaned and shook her head. She picked up her phone, said a silent prayer of thanks to have a signal, and looked up images of Adam Yorrow. Dalton polished off his beer. The sound of his chair dragging over the floor drew her attention. She stood as she watched him carry his bowl to the sink and then go for another beer.

"You want another?"

"Sure." She took another long swig of hers and crossed the room. This time Dalton opened both bottles. Journey watched him as she emptied her own bottle and set it on the counter.

"So, this is him? The guy with lips that are too red?"

Journey laughed and looked up at him as he sidled up closer to her. She took the beer he passed her without thought, without a glance, and nearly ripped her hand away from him when she felt a low hum of electric current at the brush of his fingers on hers.

"Wait." He shook his head.

Up close like this, she could smell his cologne. Something simple, but clean and fresh. Journey started to step away from him, suddenly too aware of his body brushing up against hers. She was grateful Dalton stepped closer to the table to put his beer down and then turned back to take her phone from her. Journey took the opportunity to cross her arms over her breasts. As if Dalton could magically tell her nipples had tightened with arousal just being close to him.

What the hell, Journey? Being close to Dalton McKenzie *is turning you on? Good grief, you need to get laid if your brother's kid friend has you wound up like this.*

Naturally, she'd left her vibrator at home. Who wanted to play with sex toys when they were spending a weekend at a bed and breakfast with friends? Well, who wanted to play with sex toys *alone* on a weekend like this? Odds were, Vanessa and Parker had plans to have a good time.

"What?" Dalton's voice jolted her from her thoughts.

"Nothing. Why?" She hoped she sounded nonchalant. Breathed a quiet sigh of relief when he turned his attention back to the picture on her phone.

"So, his lips are too red." He tipped his head and narrowed his eyes.

"Do you see what I mean?"

"I guess?" Dalton's frown said he didn't see what she meant. Not at all. "And, Abbott's got lips like this?"

"Yes."

"So, you didn't even kiss him."

Journey was not the blushing kind. She was a bit harsh, bold, and unapologetic about life. But when Dalton moved only his eyes to look at her, she felt a rush of heat in her cheeks.

"Well, of course, I kissed him," she mumbled. "But it… he didn't…"

"Kissing him didn't do it for you?"

"No."

"Wow. That's…" Dalton handed her phone back to her. She tapped out of the search engine and shoved it in her back pocket. "I had no idea girls thought things like that."

"Oh, come on." She groaned as she sat again to finish her soup. "There have to be things that turn you off with women."

Dalton paused, as if to consider her words. "Maybe, but not red lips."

"Okay, so, what? Share."

"I hate it when girls end every sentence in a question mark. Like they're unsure of everything they say."

"Yeah, but uptalking's not a physical thing that you don't like."

"Uptalking," he repeated and shook his head. "Um…I don't know, Journey. I don't have a thing that I don't like. I just know what I do like."

"What about women who wear glasses?"

"Sexy as hell."

"Um." She swallowed a mouthful of soup and chased it with a swallow of beer. "Freckles."

"Cute."

"Red hair."

"Feisty."

Journey snorted. "Okay, tell me what you do like."

"Tell you what sort of woman I'm attracted to?"

"Yeah."

"Strong. Independent. Someone not looking for a man to complete her. But someone who wants to share who she is, to share her life with a man."

Journey's lips twitched as she fought the grimace. Rather than comment, she ate more soup.

"What?" he finally asked. "What's wrong with that?"

"Well, nothing, if you like cheese," she answered. "And anyway—"

"Whoa, whoa, whoa." Dalton shook his head. "What does that mean?"

"Never thought I'd hear that kind of bullshit come out of your mouth." She shrugged as if it was simple. "And again, I'm talking about physical traits. What attracts you to a woman?"

"Her eyes."

"See? Was that hard? What about her eyes? Blue? You like blue eyes?"

"I like intense, honest eyes. Doesn't matter the color. I want to see her soul when she looks at me."

Journey gave a dramatic look around the kitchen.

"What're you doing?"

"Looking for some wine to go with your cheese."

"What do you want me to say?" He laughed and tossed his hands up. "That I like boobs? Of course, I do. I'm a guy."

"Lemme guess. You like big boobs."

"I like them big or small—"

"Ohmygod, Dalton! Stop it!" She rolled her eyes and took another drink. Dalton's gaze trailed her hand as she pushed her hair back from her face.

"I do. I'm a nipple guy."

"What?"

"I love the curves. All sizes." He smiled. "But I love nipples."

Journey managed to hold still, though with the heat between her legs right now, it was a hell of a job. She wanted to squirm. To scratch that little itch, the one that was beginning to throb. Her nipples tightened again as she stared at Dalton's mouth. Imagined his lips tugging at them.

"Is there really that much difference from one nipple to the next?" She took another swig of beer, aware that she was loosening up, maybe too much. Dammit all, she should have just stayed at home and waited with everyone else to drive up tomorrow.

"You'd be surprised."

4

Journey stared at him silently.

"What?" He pushed back from the table and crossed his left ankle over his right knee.

"I'm just trying to picture this." She laughed softly. "Like, I wanna go look at nudes with you so you can point out the differences."

Dalton couldn't hold in the hearty laugh. Stunned by her comment, he shook his head and gestured to her bottle with his.

"You're a lightweight."

"I'm not."

"What happened to you? You used to drink like a fish."

"Still do." She shrugged. "I'm just seriously curious now."

"You've never made out with a woman?"

"Seriously?" She jerked her head back in shock. "No. I can see why you might think that with a mother like Lenore, but no, Dalton, that's not my thing."

"Wait." He leaned forward. "What? Why would you say that?"

He had only been teasing her; but judging from the wounded look that had shadowed her face for a moment, as well as her reaction, it was obvious he'd hurt her.

"But you've watched movies with nudity."

"Yeah," she shrugged and blew him off, "hell, I've seen Van naked almost as much as I've seen myself naked. But I'm still curious about your thoughts on this."

Dalton had fantasized about Journey naked far too many times to count in his lifetime. Never Vanessa. The image of both of them naked doing God only knew what blew his mind. He stood up and paced away from the table.

"What?" Journey sounded amused. She didn't sound drunk, except that the Journey he knew would never have this conversation with him. "Thinking about Van naked gotcha hot and bothered?"

"Both of you naked," he mumbled and adjusted his dick. No way to hide his erection, so he'd settle for trying to get comfortable.

"That's dirty!" Her laugh was loud and sweet and sexy as hell. "Sorry. It's not like that with us, and she's taken, anyway."

"You wanna see what's on TV?" he asked her. "Or maybe read? I'm sure there's a Superbowl rerun on or something."

"This bothers you? Talking about nipples?"

"Journey." He ground his teeth together and turned to aim a look of warning at her.

"Like. I mean. Explain." She tipped her head at him. "Difference in color?"

"Sure."

"Taste?"

"Nope." Dalton shook his head.

"Really? We all taste the same to you?"

"Not doing this." He pushed his chair in and nodded toward the living room.

"Why's it okay for you to push me about my lip hang up, but I can't ask what you like about nipples?"

"What do you like about men?" He tossed the conversation back at her. Journey scrambled to follow him to the living room.

"Broad shoulders."

"Right."

"I do." She shrugged. "Forearms."

"What?"

Journey followed him to the couch. Dalton put his beer on the table and bit off a groan when she took his hand to push his sleeve up. He stared at her fingers as she traced them over his skin.

"Look at that. Sexy as fuck." Her voice was thick with desire.

He had to agree. Journey's plain cut fingernails and long fingers on his arm were sexy as fuck.

"Did you have something to drink before we left town?" he teased.

"No." She dropped his hand and stepped away. Their eyes met for a moment, but she jerked her gaze away before he could read her. "Sorry. I'm seriously just as curious about this as you are about my hang up with red lips."

Fire roared through his blood and exploded in his dick when she dropped her gaze to his lips.

"Too red for your taste?"

She laughed softly and shook her head. "No."

"This is dangerous." He didn't recognize the gruff voice as his own. His eyes stayed locked on her face as she nodded and stepped toward him at the same time.

"Dangerous night," she agreed. Dalton held his breath when she raised up on her tiptoes and leaned into him. Heat flared in her eyes when her middle pressed into him, hard and ready for her.

"But you kissed Abbott, and he has really red lips."

"I did." Her whisper traced a chill over his skin.

Before Dalton could think, his fingers cupped her chin. His thumb smoothed over her lips—so soft and natural. He tipped his head, felt her breath on his face, and tried to remember why this was a bad idea.

Kendric would kill him. For the conversation alone. Kissing his best friend's sister was way the hell off-limits.

Journey parted her lips. He felt the scrape of her teeth on his thumb and the head of his dick at the same time. One kiss. One kiss wouldn't hurt. Kendric would never have to know that he and his sister had had a naughty conversation and experimented with a kiss and then put the buzzing attraction thing to bed.

Rest.

Not bed.

No thinking about beds right now.

"Are you gonna kiss me?" he asked her.

"Maybe I'm waiting for permission."

"I think you know you've got it, Journey."

She touched his lips with hers. A soft, barely there touch strong enough to bring him to his knees. Maybe this was a one-time thing, one kiss, but Dalton wasn't going to settle for that. If he was going to steal a kiss from his best friend's sister, he was going to kiss the fuck out of her before he let her walk away.

Journey didn't seem in any hurry to move away from him, though. He snuck a peek at her, shocked to find her eyes closed. She struck him as the type of woman who would watch. Like, she would watch every second if he undressed her and went down on her to kiss her core.

The hesitation. The second, soft brush of her lips over his. The sweet sigh that warmed his face. Jesus. She was going to break him.

With a kiss.

The house was silent around them, and a blustery wind batted at the windows, and outside snow and ice fell fast and hard. But inside, it was cozy and warm, and the one woman Dalton had truly ever wanted was kissing him. Soft, curious kisses. A little bit playful, a little bit tender.

Everything he never thought she would be.

Dalton had expected Journey to be just as greedy and exact with kissing and sex as she was with the rest of her life. These soft, sweet kisses threw him off-guard, caught him in places other than his dick. He wanted to touch her. God, yes, he had wanted to touch every inch of Journey Ryan's body for years.

But this. *Tonight.* The peek behind those walls people normally had to scale to see her. The kissing.

This might hurt.

"You're not kissing me back." She tipped her head back and opened her eyes.

"It's your show," he told her.

The shadow touched her face again, the one from the

kitchen. Dalton wanted to stop her. Even though she moved in to kiss him again, he wanted to stop her. And talk. He wanted to ask what haunted her, because he felt it in the room with them, too.

Her lips were more persuasive this time. Hungry. The flick of her tongue over the center of his upper lip rocked him. Unsteady on his feet, Dalton reached for her hips and yanked her hard against his middle. She traced his lips with her velvety, hot tongue, and when Dalton still didn't give in, she nipped at him and caught his lower lip in her teeth.

"Jesus!" he hissed. Journey struck with finesse, her tongue sliding quickly into his mouth and stroking his. And then, that quickly, she slowed her lips to those soft, sweet kisses again. Tongues dancing and stroking, lips touching and parting and touching again.

Dalton's head was spinning, his heart thumping wildly in his chest when she broke the kiss and stepped away from him. He had fantasized about rough, dirty sex with her so often, it was a shock to be so turned on by her sweetness. Her gentle sighs and the light press of her body to his.

Trouble was now he didn't just want to fuck her.

He wanted to love her.

She might have turned on the innocence and charm for the kiss, but Dalton wasn't stupid enough to believe a woman like Journey would really want him.

"Guys with really red lips don't kiss like that." She shook her head.

Dalton stared after her as she crossed the room to the staircase.

"Like what?" he called when she was halfway up.

"They don't kiss me and turn me on." She shrugged and turned away to head upstairs.

5

They'd claimed their rooms as Sylvia walked them through the house, so Journey hurried to hers, closed the door, and rested against it.

"What the hell, Journey?"

Her hiss was supposed to be angry, but even she thought she sounded desperate. Dalton had never been anything more than a pain-in-the-ass friend of her brother's and a sort of friend she talked to now and then as they got older. While she'd always liked him, she hadn't ever been attracted to him.

And as long as she was being honest, she might as well admit that this felt bigger than that. Journey didn't date much. She didn't do romance. No candle lit dinners or Valentine's Day roses. She hooked up with who she needed, when she needed to. She had seen enough of her friends' relationships go south, not to mention the weird dynamic between her own parents, to want or believe in love.

So, what the hell was up with this fluttery feeling about Dalton?

"Weird night," she mumbled. She pushed off the door, gave herself a mental shake, and grabbed her duffel bag from the floor. Within minutes, she had changed from her jeans to sweats, from her blouse to a loose sweatshirt, and rearranged her hair in yet another messy bun. She thought about taking her makeup off, but she wanted to quell this ridiculous sexual tension between them. Not scare the hell out of him.

Leaving the partially smudged eyeliner and the creased shadow as it was, Journey grabbed her book and went back downstairs. Her knees were still wobbly, but she forced herself to offer Dalton—who was now kicked back on the couch with the TV on—a cool smile. As if kissing him hadn't sent her stupid heart—the one she would have sworn she didn't have—all topsy-turvy.

"Find a Superbowl rerun?" she asked him.

"No, but they have Netflix, and I found a show to watch with that guy in it."

Crossing the room to join him on the couch, Journey cast a cautious look at the TV. Sure enough, there was Adam Yarrow's pale face and red lips on the screen. Her groan turned into a laugh as she dropped to sit, sure to keep a few feet between them.

"He doesn't turn you on?" Dalton's frown did things to her. To her belly. Her throat. Her girl stuff. When he caught her staring at him instead of the TV, she cleared her throat and shrugged.

"That's the weird thing," she mumbled, figuring she might as well go with the flow, because Dalton wasn't going to let it go. "He does. He's a really good-looking guy. I just don't like his lips."

"So." Dalton tipped the corner of his mouth up. "By extension, you think Abbott's hot, but you don't like his lips."

"Abbott's hot, sure," she agreed, "but I'm not into him. At all."

Dalton studied her face silently and finally nodded. She waited for him to say something, but he only turned back to aim the remote at the TV.

"No. Nope." Journey tossed her book on the battered coffee table and scooted toward him to grab the remote when the scene unpaused and began to play. "You keep bringing this up and then, like, blowing it off when I answer you."

"Told you I'm curious."

"So, what? You're using me to research a woman's thoughts?"

"Not exactly."

"Then what?"

She tugged the remote from his hand and pushed pause again. He watched her toss it aside but didn't answer her.

"You started this," she reminded him.

With a long sigh, he raised his arms over his head to stretch. Heat scorched through her body, straight from her heart to her core, when he let his gaze take a long, slow stroll over her.

"Dalton."

"Dric sent a text when you were upstairs."

Journey tried to swallow, but her mouth was bone dry. She nodded, because she knew without him saying a word that her brother had decided to wait until morning to make the drive. Which meant that she and Dalton would be alone together at Kristophe House all night.

"We probably shouldn't do this." Her voice was gruff with lust and uncertainty. Lust she was familiar with. Uncertainty, not so much. Not with her sex life. She was torn with disgust at that vulnerability Dalton created within her and a strange need to explore that pit in her belly. Would he fill it? If she climbed on top of him right now and rode him until they were both spent and satiated, would he fill that emptiness in her belly?

No one else had ever been able to make her feel complete. Why would Dalton McKenzie be any different?

"Probably not."

Maybe it was the defeat in his voice. Maybe it was the searching look in his eyes. Maybe it was the memory of his hard cock pressed against her middle. Journey moved. Slowly. Not catlike. Not seductively.

Cautiously.

She inched closer to him, starved suddenly for his affection and terrified of what it meant. What it would bring.

Dalton's arms came around her as she crawled over him to straddle his lap.

"I want to," she whispered. "I want to do this."

Eyes locked with his, she sank her teeth into her lower lip and waited for him to move. To say yes. Rather than the kiss she wanted, Dalton smoothed her hair back from her face and traced her cheekbones with his fingertips with a gentle, tender touch for such a big man.

"I want you to want me." She leaned closer and wedged his erection between her thighs. Dalton's eyes flashed with heat. Eyes open, she kissed him, a soft press of her dry lips to his.

"You know I want you." He moved his hands to her hips and squeezed as he raised his hips to grind against her.

She sat back, eyes on his lips. She wanted his mouth on hers again. She wanted those kisses they shared earlier. But she wanted him to do it. To make the moves. He seemed too content to react to her, to let her lead. Usually, she would demand and take control.

But tonight. Dalton.

It was different.

"Do you?" She eased the elastic of her sweatshirt up slowly. The air was cold on her bare skin, but Dalton's hot gaze chased away the chill.

"I'm fucked."

His surrender danced over her skin like fire, and her nipples tightened as she bared her breasts to him and pulled the shirt off over her head. Seemingly dazed by her partial nudity, Dalton drank her in with adoration and lust. When he finally moved, the stroke of his fingers over her bare back raised chill bumps over her skin. Her nipples beaded so tight, they ached.

He raised his head from the couch and pulled her hips closer. And there was that kiss again. Tender and curious. Only this time, Journey was uncovered, bared to him, in more ways than one. The touch of his hands on her back, the scrape of her sensitive nipples over his thermal T, the warmth of his lips against hers drove her mad for more.

And yet, she loved the slow, painful torture. The waiting. The hope that any second, he would cup her breasts. Touch her nipples with those gentle fingers.

"I love kissing you," she whispered. For a moment, they hesitated. His hands still roaming her back, their lips parted, yet barely touching. Journey gasped softly at the stroke of his tongue inside her mouth and whimpered when he pulled back just enough to break the contact.

"I never imagined it would be like this with you."

Fingers splayed over his cheek now, she met his eyes. What did that mean?

"You've thought about this? Before?"

"Fuck, yes, I've thought about this."

Could he see her erratic pulse in her neck? Her heart raced at his admission. No longer her brother's friend, Dalton was a man who knew her and wanted her. She pressed her lips together and ran her fingers over his soft blond hair.

"What do you want it to be like?"

"Just exactly like this."

She moaned with pleasure when he trailed his fingers over her waistband and pressed them between her breasts. His knuckles brushed her curves.

"Any way you want it, Journey."

Journey curled her fingers around the back of his neck, eyes drawn to his mouth. She snuggled closer and flattened her breasts against his chest. Dalton turned his hand, finally cupping her, weighing her breast in his hand. He pressed his thumb to her nipple but moved his other hand up to push his fingers into her hair. She yelped softly when he tugged the elastic from the bun but moved willingly when he captured her mouth for another kiss.

"I want you to make love to me."

She whisper-moaned the words into his mouth, the fire in her body raging from the pressure of his cock between her legs, his fingers now rolling, pinching her nipple.

"Make me come, Dalton." She trailed kisses from his lips over his cheek and then nipped at his earlobe. "I want you to make me come."

"Shh." He turned his head, his mouth searching for hers again. This kiss was deeper, wet and hot. Hungry. Still tender, but Journey felt the demand in the way his tongue curled around hers and stroked. "I promise, Journey. Anything for you."

"Please." She kissed him. "Now. Here."

"Hold on." He stood easily, still holding her in his arms.

Journey wrapped her legs around his waist, but she pressed her cheek to his and shook her head.

"Right here, Dalton. Please."

"I've got you." He swept his tongue inside her lips again as he squatted at the couch and lowered her to lie before him. "Hold on, J. I've got you."

Eyes locked with his, Journey moaned and gasped with pleasure, with anticipation, when Dalton slipped his hands inside her sweats and panties and pushed the front low with his thumbs, baring only the small triangle of her dark curls.

"Oh god." She panted, already out of breath, as he brushed his thumb down over her and finally touched her core.

"Are you sure?"

Kneeling before her, dark eyes on hers, he waited.

"Yes."

Stunned at his speed, that he hadn't moved except to duck his head between her legs, Journey dipped her chin to watch him. Her sweats and panties still covering everything but the spot where Dalton kissed her, she palmed the back of his head and concentrated on the slick heat of his tongue and the tug of his lips.

"Dalton."

She needed the release, the waves of warm pleasure that lapped low at her body. The unfurling, the explosion in her belly, the pain of holding back.

"Too fast," she whispered. "Not yet."

"Let go, Journey," he commanded. "I've got you. And we've got the whole night to do this."

As if he sensed that she still fought the urge to unravel at his licking, his sucking, Dalton eased a finger inside her and scraped his teeth over her most sensitive spot, sending her heart and soul crashing over the edge.

"Dalton!" she screamed, unable to hold on any longer. Feet on the couch, her thighs at his cheeks, she lifted her hips to take more of him as her heart soared, and tears streaked her face.

"Hold on," he whispered.

Jesus. He had wrecked her. Limp like a ragdoll in a pit bull's teeth, she squeezed her eyes closed and let the pleasure roll over her, the aftershocks of the orgasm as sweetly painful as that first wild rush of pleasure.

"Hold on, Journey," he said again.

What more could she do? Helpless at the moment without him, she stroked her hands over his head and held on.

6

Journey, wrecked before him on the sofa, panted softly in the aftermath of her orgasm. Dalton wanted more. Skin. Touches. Her hands on him. More kissing. More confessions about how badly he wanted to wreck her again, how badly he wanted to bury himself inside her and make love to her—mostly, he wanted to hear her begging him for more. But he hesitated, worried now that the Journey Ryan he had grown up with would regret what they had started.

"Wow." Her whisper puffed him up inside for a moment, but when she didn't add anything, worry crushed the hope.

Because he wanted to slide her sweats down her legs and take his time easing her panties over her feet and admire her smooth thighs and her flat belly and she hadn't yet moved or said more than *wow*, he simply pressed a chaste kiss low on her belly and lifted his head to look at her. Eyes closed and lashes on her cheeks, she looked angelic. Except that her nude breasts and the flush in her cheeks looked a little pornographic. Dalton liked both angles, both sides.

She moaned quietly—in protest, he hoped—when he loosened his hold on her. He stroked his fingers over her hips and let her sweats slide back up a bit toward her waist.

"Dalton." She cupped the back of his head when he trailed staccato kisses over her belly.

"Hmm?"

"What're you doing?" Still whispering, she pressed her fingertips to the back of his neck. "Why did you stop?"

"You wanted me to make you come," he reminded her.

"Is that all I get?"

"You tell me what you want, Journey." He pressed his knuckle against the curve of her breast.

"I want to be with you."

From his angle, he saw her struggle to swallow, noticed she was still panting lightly. Their eyes met, Journey's bright and hot.

"Are you sure?"

"You don't want to do this?" She pushed herself up to her elbows and eyed him with panic. "What? Are you worried about Kendric?"

"I don't wanna talk about Kendric after what I just did to you." He shook his head. "I told you I've thought about being with you like this a lot." He smoothed his knuckle over her breast and flicked her nipple with his fingertip. "And for the record, your nipples are perfect."

Her soft laugh eased the fire of worry in his gut.

"You haven't even tasted them."

"I think it's safe to say I love the way you taste," he said around a grin, "but I would love to get my mouth on the rest of you."

"Should we go upstairs?"

Dalton didn't care if they were buck naked and rocking the house and the rest of their group—including Kendric—walked in to find them making love. But maybe she preferred to go up to a bedroom.

"Yes."

Dalton worked out daily, so while some of his bulk had softened a bit from too much beer and pizza, he was still in good shape. He moved with ease to stand and then offered Journey a hand.

"Doesn't feel so sexy when we have to get up and walk up the stairs," she mumbled. "Why don't they show the unsexy stuff in the movies?"

"It's not in the books, either," he told her. "C'mere."

Longing stabbed through him when she went to him without hesitation. He had never imagined such an intimate side of Journey, and he had to remind himself tonight wasn't real. They weren't a couple. They weren't making love; they weren't going to wake up in the morning and realize they were *in love*. They were spending a snowy, cozy night together and enjoying each other's company. And bodies.

Absolutely nothing wrong with that, as long as he didn't let himself get carried away with his stupid teenage daydreams.

"What're you doing?"

A low rumble of laughter bubbled up from her belly; Dalton felt it when he slipped his arms around her.

"Kissing you," he told her.

Journey tipped her head back and threw her arms over his shoulders. "This is more like it."

"Better than the way I just kissed you?"

"God, no." She grinned and pressed her forehead to his chest. "Before that. It was like you didn't want to kiss me."

Dalton smoothed his hands over her back to cup her ass cheeks. Instinctively, Journey lifted her legs and wrapped them around his waist. Again, he felt her body shake with laughter when he started toward the stairs.

"What're you—" she snorted as he took the first stair and kept going. "Seriously, Dalton? You're gonna carry me upstairs?"

"It's sexier, isn't it?"

"Well, yeah," she admitted as she tightened her legs around his waist and burrowed her face into his neck. "I love it, but I'm not a lightweight."

"You're right." He squeezed her butt and laughed when she squealed. "You must weigh a hundred pounds."

"Dalton." She snorted, but she shifted in his arms and tipped her head to the side. Rather than say more, she nibbled on his neck.

"Your room or mine?"

"Do you have condoms on you right this minute?"

"In my wallet," he told her.

"'kay." She kissed his cheek. "My room. It's closer."

They had only just arrived at the bed and breakfast, but her room already smelled faintly of her perfume. Dalton noticed her open duffel bag on the floor at the foot of the bed. The peek at a T-shirt and denim stirred more than his dick. Messing around with Journey Ryan was a bad idea.

And that bad idea had nothing to do with what his best

friend would think about him getting his sister into bed. Journey stirred in his arms, and her soft little curves snug against him drove all rational thought from his mind. She was all in; there was no reason the two of them shouldn't share this night together doing whatever they wanted.

Thoughts of her body under his downstairs on the sofa, of the way her body had reacted to his touch, emboldened him now. Greedy to taste her, to slide his tongue over hers, to claim every part of her, Dalton kissed her with hunger and tenderness, thrilling at the way she kissed him back.

Her arms still around his neck, she unlocked her ankles at his waist and slid her legs down over his hips. When that kiss ended and slipped right into another, Journey moved her hands to his arms.

"I wanna touch you," she half kissed, half whispered. "Take it off."

Dalton tugged his shirt over his head, dropped it to the floor, and turned his attention to her hands on the waist-band of his jeans. Their eyes met as she unbuckled his belt. Dalton kicked out of his jeans with ease, but he plucked her off her feet again and laid her down on the bed before she had a chance to finish undressing.

"Wait," he told her.

Pinned under him, her breasts smashed under his chest, she eyed him with wonder.

"How does this go?" She pressed her fingers to his lips. "When you think about doing this with me? How does it go?"

"You don't really wanna know, Journey."

"I do."

"You on top."

"Is that what you want?"

"I think I want everything. Every way. Every naughty thing I've ever done." He took her hands and pushed them gently to the bed over her head. "With you."

"Me, too."

"I wanna make this so good for you, you forget any other guy who's been inside you."

A lazy smile touched her lips.

"This is crazy." She tried to move her hands, but he shook his head.

"Do you ever—"

"Well, no, because you were a scrawny little kid when I really knew you." She bit her lip. "And it's different with you."

"Different how?"

She closed her eyes for a second and then arched her eyebrows. "I don't go to bed with guys I like. Sex is just… physical. And I don't sleep with anyone."

"Are you telling me at some point you're gonna kick me out of your bed?"

"No." She lifted her head from the bed to kiss him. "I'm saying it's different, because I want you to sleep with me tonight."

Dalton pressed his open mouth to her neck as she shifted on her back to allow him closer. He might have imagined Journey as a wildcat in bed, and he supposed there were times when she was. But he loved the slower, mellow pace, the exploration of her body, and her investigation of his body. Her hands were gentle, though her touch wasn't shy.

They moved like lovers who had been together forever, though soft sighs of pleasure and surprise escaped her lips several times. When it was over, Dalton slept better with her pressed to his side than he had since leaving Texas.

He awoke around midnight and slipped out of bed, hoping he wouldn't disturb her.

"Where are you going?"

Her whispered question stopped him in the middle of hobbling to get his jeans on.

"To turn everything off downstairs. Make sure the door's locked."

Journey, still nude—though now her skin was marked by his teeth and the five o'clock shadow on his face—propped herself up on her elbow and eyed him with suspicion.

"You're coming back?"

Dalton turned to her as he pulled his jeans just over his hips. Fly open, his dick already straining again at the sight of her there, waiting for him.

"Two minutes."

Her smile was enough to do him in. He leaned over the bed, propped one hand on the headboard and cupped her chin in the other.

"Need anything?"

"I brought cookies."

"You want cookies?" He certainly hadn't expected that.

"With you. Here." She shrugged. "Naked. Why not?"

"Minute and a half," he promised. Her laughter followed him out the door. Downstairs, he turned the TV off and fished around in a picnic basket—who would have thought Journey Ryan would have a picnic basket?—to find a container of homemade cookies. They would need something to drink, and as good as milk would be with homemade cookies of any sort, it didn't seem to fit the occasion. With a chuckle, Dalton grabbed two longnecks from the cooler, turned the kitchen lights off, and headed back through the living room.

"You're taking too long! Get up here!"

Journey's good-natured demand made him laugh. And move faster. He locked the front door, turned the lamp off in the living room, and hustled up the stairs again.

"Mm." Flat on her back again, Journey rolled her head on her pillow to look at him. The lazy grin she gave him when she saw the longneck bottles hooked in his fingers made his heart hurt. "Can I ask for a favor?"

"Sure." He handed the bottles to her, set the cookies down, and kicked out of his jeans. "What kind of favor?"

When she didn't answer him, he tossed his jeans aside and looked at her to find her eyes on his hips. On the proof of his arousal.

"Sexual." She licked her lips and cleared her throat.

"What haven't we covered yet?" He moved the cookies aside and climbed into bed beside her.

"Actually, I'm kind of interested in a repeat performance."

Dalton took a bottle from her, twisted the top off, and then traded her for the other one.

"Okay." He nodded. "Of which act? Foreplay? Intercourse?"

Journey took a long drink of her beer and handed it to him. Dalton put the bottles aside on the nightstand and turned back to her. She leaned into him, smoothed her hand up over his cheek, and kissed him with the same passion she'd shown him all night.

"All of it." Her warm whispered words touched his lower lip and his chin.

"I would be happy to do that for you."

She drew back to look at him, the skin around her eyes crinkled with laughter.

"Could you do it now?"

"What about the cookies?"

"I'll give you a cookie for every orgasm you give me."

"You owe me about four already," he reminded her.

"I made two dozen."

Dalton scooped her up to straddle his hips.

"Hold on."

"Not this time." She shook her head. "You better hold on this time. I'm feeling a little wild, Dalton McKenzie."

ourney hadn't lied to Dalton. She couldn't remember the last time she spent an entire night in bed with someone. Other than the girls' nights when she and Vanessa were either too drunk or just too tired to go home and ended up staying over. Those nights were nothing like sleeping with Dalton, obviously. After all, Journey and Dalton spent the small hours nude, curled around each other's bodies.

She had no idea what had come over her the night before, but as she pulled herself up through the haze of sleep and dreams, she realized she didn't regret it. No, she didn't envision herself in a relationship with Dalton—ever—but she didn't exactly regret being with him, being so intimate with him. The slow, tender lovemaking at first—definitely not her style. And though she was surprised to realize how good it felt to be cherished rather than ravished, she didn't want it to be like that again with anyone else.

The smell of coffee stirred her from thoughts of the

night before. Wondering who had come inside while they slept, Journey turned to Dalton's side of the bed, shocked to find it empty. Still nude, but still deliciously warm from the way his hands had clothed her through the night, she smoothed her hand over the cool sheet and remembered the hard muscles under his warm skin.

He had made her laugh. Not many men could do that. Journey didn't want other men to make her laugh. She didn't want anything from men other than the obvious. And she didn't even need that so often anymore.

But last night? What the hell? He had teased her, ribbed her on the drive last night about her date at her dad's party. Dalton had always needled her about boys and flirting and kissing and all of the stuff little brothers teased their older sisters and their friends about. When they were younger, it made her mad just because she didn't want the attention. Lenore was the attention grabber in the family; no room at all for Journey in the spotlight with her mother there. And more importantly, she didn't *want* to be like her mother.

Years later, when Kendric and Dalton were in college and Dalton would come back home now and then for parties, he still ribbed her, though he was more subtle. It was in his tone when he commented on who she was running around with, rather than the things he said. When he was thirteen, he commented on her outfits—easy-access tops, for instance—and when he was in college, he would simply eyeball her flavor of the night and roll his eyes. Maybe ask if she was with someone and put a sarcastic spin on the name.

But last night, it hadn't made her mad. It felt more like flirting. Which was weird in itself since she didn't flirt.

And maybe it shouldn't have come as a surprise to her when Dalton confessed to fantasizing about her, but it had. Maybe not when he was fourteen or fifteen, because isn't that what boys that age did twenty-four seven? But the college version of Dalton? The adult version of Dalton? Thinking about undressing her and doing the things they had done last night? That had blown her away.

Chills racked her body at the memory of the things they had done last night. She wanted more. Not only had she never spent an entire night with a guy, sleeping in his arms, she had never awoken with the desire for more.

No. She didn't want to *date* him. Did she? She just wanted more of what they had shared last night. More of the teasing and the talking—about their lives, his worry over his dad and her nonexistent relationship with her mother. More hanging out over a cold beer, watching TV. More kissing and skin.

Damn. That sounded like how Vanessa talked about Parker. And *they* were dating. Well, now they were more than dating.

Dalton was downstairs making coffee for her. Maybe even breakfast. She could go downstairs, and they could sip their coffee by the Christmas tree and even make love again on the sofa or somewhere in the kitchen. Or maybe he was going to sneak back up here with coffee and breakfast.

Breakfast in bed would be another new experience for her.

She laughed softly as she sat up and examined the sheet for cookie crumbs. They did eat cookies sometime through the night. Dalton must have taken the cookie container and the empty beer bottles downstairs with him.

Journey didn't want to spend another second up here alone. She slipped out of bed, shivering in the cold room. As much as she would like to appear downstairs in the kitchen with him just as she was right now, it was too cold. She used the restroom quickly, washed her hands and face, and brushed her teeth. Then she found her sweats—the same ones Dalton had taken off her last night —and slipped them on. When she realized her sweatshirt was still downstairs, she grabbed a long-sleeved T-shirt from her duffle bag and yanked it on. The material was dark and loose enough that if anyone should arrive while she was downstairs, he or she wouldn't notice she wasn't wearing a bra unless they looked really closely.

She grabbed her phone as she hurried out of her room. The sounds of the season greeted her—no, it wasn't Bing, but Dalton had Christmas music playing in the kitchen. Dean Martin was singing "Marshmallow World." A weird, warm holiday thrill streaked through her as her toes hit the top step. When her phone buzzed in her hand, she answered it without looking at the screen.

"Hello?"

"Hey. Journey."

"What's going on?" Journey slowed on the steps. Vanessa didn't sound upset, not like something was wrong. But sort of…guilty.

Like she and Parker weren't coming to Kristophe House at all now. Journey hated the thought of the fun weekend with friends going out the window, but after last night, she didn't mind the thought of being tucked up away here alone with Dalton for the rest of the weekend. What would he think about that?

She was pretty sure if it was just the two of them for the weekend, he would be as happy about that as she was. Two more nights of hanging out with him. Maybe playing games. Watching Christmas movies. Playing other kinds of games. Sleeping all tangled up together in bed again.

But what if Kendric and Erin showed up? Would Dalton feel weird sleeping with her? Surely, they wouldn't just mess around in the open, would they? Would Dalton want to sneak around, though? Would he lie by omission to Kendric? *Would she?* Nothing about her private life, her sex life, had ever been up for discussion with Dric, but then again, Dalton was his best friend. That made everything different.

"Listen, Parker and I…"

Journey felt a pang in her chest. She slowed again in the middle of the staircase.

"You what?"

"We decided maybe we'd just stay home. Um. We're gonna babysit Mase and Eli, so Nick and Cedes can do some last-minute Christmas shopping and last-minute wedding stuff."

Vanessa gushed everything out so fast, it sounded like one giant word. Like she was worried Journey was going to be angry with her.

"But you and Parker? You're okay?"

"We're fine."

Journey lowered herself to sit on the step third from the bottom.

"Like fine, like he just delivered you breakfast in bed and topped it off with a couple of orgasms and you're going to pick out names today? Or fine…like…that weird we're just friends who made a baby together fine?"

"Fine." Vanessa sounded funny, a little out of breath. "We are *so* good."

"My God, he's not topping your breakfast off right now, is he?"

"No. We've been done for at least five minutes."

Journey snorted. "I love that. I actually like him. This is huge, Van."

"Oh, I know. *Journey Ryan* approves of my man."

"You should get married."

"Maybe someday."

"Before that baby comes along," Journey said quietly, no longer teasing. "I know things have changed since we were kids. But if you love each other, why not get married?"

"He hasn't asked me yet."

"So, take him by the balls and ask him."

"Hmm." Vanessa chuckled. "Maybe I will."

"I'll call you when I'm home."

"You could call me before you come home."

"You'll be busy."

"You're not mad?" Vanessa whined.

"Nope. It's good."

"How was last night? Been a while since you were stuck with Dric and Dalton in the same room."

Journey laughed softly.

"I thought I heard you out here." Dalton appeared in the kitchen doorway. He leaned on the frame, arms folded over his chest. Journey eyed the green thermal tee he wore with a different pair of jeans than those he had on last night. He had showered already. Bummer.

"It was good." No need to go into details right now. She didn't have time for the questions Vanessa would most definitely ask.

"Okay. Love you."

"You, too." Journey ended the call, eyes on Dalton. "You showered without me?"

She heard his low, long groan across the room.

"I wasn't sure how you would feel about last night." He shrugged.

"Really?"

"In the light of day," he mumbled. "I made coffee."

She nodded. "You could bring it upstairs."

The grin that touched his lips made her shiver with anticipation. But before either of them could move, someone pounded on the door. Journey wondered if it was Sylvia coming to check on them or if Dric and Erin had arrived.

Dalton crossed the room to get the door as Journey stood, prepared to get her own coffee.

"Hey!"

She stopped by the sofa when she heard her brother's voice.

"Hey, man." Dalton nodded. Journey watched with amusement when they did the bro hug.

"Let the weekend begin!" Kendric stepped aside to usher Erin inside. Followed by a short, curvy redhead. Erin pressed into Kendric, and the redhead eyed Dalton appreciatively. "Dalton, this is Lacy. Lacy, my friend Dalton."

Dalton offered the redhead a smile, but he lifted his eyes to look for Journey.

Ouch. Boy had she misunderstood her brother's plans for the weekend!

Careful not to step on her heart, Journey lifted her hand in a half-hearted wave and turned away from them.

"Hey, J!" Kendric called. "You look like you just rolled out of bed."

Journey considered throat punching him. Flipping him off. Telling him to go to hell. But she didn't do any of the above. Because then Dalton would know.

Sex had always been physical for her, so she had never felt the sting of being used. Now she did. She didn't react now, because Dalton would know he had hurt her. And she wasn't about to let him see that.

"I'm on vacation, Dric," she called over her shoulder as she hurried back up the steps. "How were the roads?"

"Good. All cleared," he answered, completely oblivious to the knife in her throat.

Good to know. Once upstairs, she locked her bedroom door behind her and took a quick shower. Twenty minutes later, she was back downstairs, duffel bag packed and on her shoulder. As per Sylvia's instructions last night, Journey had taken the sheets from her bed, and now she ducked into the mudroom off the back porch and dropped them unceremoniously into the washer. She tried not to listen to her brother and his friends—that's all Dalton was, after all, right? *Kendric's friend?*—as she jabbed at the digital screen to select the cycle and clean level she wanted. Hard not to hear Dric and Dalton, though. Their voices had always cut through the other noise in a house. It drove her nuts when she was younger and the two of them were playing video games in the basement and yelling at the games and each other when she was trying to study or have a phone conversation or sleep.

Turned out, not much had changed, because listening to the laughter and the puffed-up testosterone coming from the kitchen had her neck and back so tight, she was afraid moving too quickly might break something. Eyes fixed on the water pouring over the gray sheets she and Dalton had made love on—scratch that, the sheets they had sex on—Journey listened to her brother deliver a punchline that apparently had both girls in stitches. For just a second, she strained to hear Dalton's voice. Had he really taken her to bed last night knowing Kendric was bringing him a toy for the weekend? Worse yet, what if he and that girl started dating and ended up getting serious, and Journey had to swallow the guilt when she was a guest at his wedding?

She snorted. The idea of Dalton getting married wasn't ridiculous. Not at all. He said he wanted to settle down and have a family. But Journey knew she was being melodramatic, worrying over that possibility with the girl Kendric had just delivered to Dalton.

Satisfied that the washer was going to do its thing, Journey closed the top and steeled herself with a deep breath. Walking out now shouldn't be a big deal. This is what she did. Years of practice, years of guarding her heart. She knew how to walk away.

Except she hadn't ever looked at it that way. She had never made a conscious decision to guard her heart. Rather, she told herself she wasn't interested in getting involved with someone. Who needed another person to worry about when it came to dinner time? What woman wanted to share her bathroom with a man? What woman wanted to have a TV blaring football or NASCAR in the background while she tried to relax with a book or soak in the tub?

Journey certainly hadn't wanted to deal with any of that.

Damn Dalton McKenzie for making her think for just one night that maybe she did.

Still, she could do this. She huffed out another big breath, stood up straight, and strolled casually into the kitchen. Erin was parked at the long table with Dric—the same table she and Dalton had sat at last night. The redhead was perched on the counter near the dishwasher; Dalton stood at the far side of the kitchen, propped against the refrigerator as if he was guarding it.

"Hey." He flashed her a smile when he saw her. "You didn't get your coffee."

"I'm good." She upped his smile with her signature blow-off grin and shook her head.

"What're you doing?" He tipped his head when he realized she was carrying her duffel bag.

"Gimme your keys, Dric."

She sounded cool and collected. There was no way anyone in the room would know she had given a piece of her heart to Dalton last night, that the two of them had blown through half a box of condoms. Inside, though, she was a little bit wrecked, and she had to remind herself to stand still, because her leg wanted to bounce.

"What?"

"Van called a few minutes before you guys got here."

"Everything okay?" Kendric shoved his chair back to stand and turn to her.

"Yeah, but they're not coming now."

"Why not?"

"Babysitting, so Nick and Cedes can get some last-minute stuff done."

"Nick's Parker's brother? The guy getting married?"

"Yep."

Dalton's gazed burned a hole in her as she watched Kendric pull his keys from his pocket.

"But why are you leaving?"

"Walk me out," she told him as she snatched his keys. "Do you really think I wanna hang out like this? I'm too old to be a fifth wheel around you guys."

She didn't look to see if Dalton heard her, but she didn't try to keep her voice down, either. Kendric followed her as she walked out of the kitchen. She called a general goodbye to the rest of them and kept her face neutral as she and Kendric approached the door.

"You just got here," her brother reminded her.

"I know. And last night was nice. It was nice to relax. Catch up a bit with Dalton." She shrugged at Kendric and glanced toward the kitchen again. "But I have no interest in hanging out with you guys and your weekend toys."

"Who says it's like that?"

"I know you guys." She winked at him. "Have Dalton swing by my place when you get back in town so you can get your Jeep."

"Journey, you don't have to—"

"I told Van I'd help her with the kids," she lied.

Kendric sighed and scrubbed his hand over his longish black curls.

"'kay." With that not-happy-but-you're-stubborn look on his face, Kendric looked so much like their father, Journey almost laughed. Deciding she should get out before Dalton came after her—as if he would—she bit down on the laugh and pulled the door open. "Be careful."

"Yep." She nodded as she stepped outside. "You, too, little brother. Do you have enough condoms for two nights?"

She took the porch steps quickly and glanced back over her shoulder to find Kendric flipping her off. She laughed.

Unless Dalton had another box of condoms in his bag, Lacy wasn't going to get near as much of him per night as Journey had.

8

Dalton watched Kendric closely when he moseyed back into the kitchen, though he pretended not to. He also checked the door several times, quickly so Kendric wouldn't catch him, to see if Journey would change her mind and come back.

Well, that was wishful thinking. Journey had just strolled out of the house with her overnight bag and Kendric's keys. She wasn't making a beer run like she had done so many times for him and Kendric back in the day. She was leaving.

So much for thinking last night meant anything to her. Granted, this—Dric showing up with his girlfriend and a spare for Dalton—didn't look good. But she could have *asked* him about it. If she was upset with him, she could have asked to talk to him rather than just storming out the door and taking off.

That was the thing, though. She didn't *storm out*.

Dalton had seen Journey pissed off at the world, but never at a man. She was ruthlessly protective of her brother, of her friends—especially Vanessa—but she had never cared enough about any one guy to be hurt or angry.

She had given him that cocky grin and turned down his reminder to get coffee. Not even an hour after she had eyed him up and down and shared her disappointment that he hadn't waited for her to shower with him. Journey didn't want anything more than what they had shared last night, so of course, she was happy to split this morning and leave Dalton spinning.

And pretending that nothing had happened with his best friend's sister.

"That the way you Texas people do breakfast?" Kendric nodded his head at the coffee maker. "Where's the bacon and grits and hash browns?"

Dalton bristled, angry with Kendric for showing up just when he had. Angry that he brought Lacy along. When he mentioned finding another friend to hang out with them this weekend, Dalton had told him no. He hadn't come home looking for a handout, and he hadn't come to Kristophe House for a meaningless hookup—although, it seemed that was exactly what he got anyway.

"Do you even know what grits are?" Dalton rolled his eyes.

"Do you have breakfast stuff?" Lacy asked from her spot on the counter.

She was cute; Dalton would admit that much. She seemed nice, though it was early in the game to really know much about her. And though Dalton didn't want to hurt her, he didn't want her. Period. Not like that.

Because she was a little too tall and curvy. Her hair wasn't black. She didn't have that snippy tone he had come to like, to listen for, when he talked to women. Lacy had some very nice curves, and if Journey asked, Dalton would tell her he assumed Lacy had beautiful breasts and nipples, too. But she wasn't Journey Ryan, so he wasn't interested.

"We do." Dalton nodded.

"Great." Lacy jumped off the counter and smoothed her hands over her hips. "Everybody move out of the way. Give me some room."

Dalton eyed her curiously. When she noticed, she laughed and shrugged. "I like to cook."

"Sounds good."

"Did you and Journey pick out bedrooms?" Kendric asked. Dalton, back to the table, nearly swallowed his tongue. He bit off a curse, relieved he wasn't about to take a drink of hot coffee, and let his mind wander briefly back to he and Journey christening the room she had chosen for the weekend.

"Yeah." He cleared his throat. "She picked the first one on the landing. I'm two doors down."

"Erin, let's go find a room."

Dalton fought the urge to call after his buddy and give him hell. First, he showed up just as Dalton was trying to feel Journey out on the previous night and whether she had regrets. Then he introduced another woman into the mix—a very pretty woman and he knew that didn't go unnoticed by Journey—and now that they had chased Journey away, Dric was heading upstairs with his girl-friend and leaving him alone with Lacy.

The very pretty, sexy woman Dric had picked out for him. The one Dalton wasn't interested in. Because she wasn't Journey.

"So." Lacy pulled the refrigerator door open and surveyed the groceries available. Dalton watched her pull out a carton of eggs, a pack of bacon, and the jug of orange juice. "Tell me you don't want grits, because I don't know what they are or how to fix them."

"Bacon and eggs is plenty." He nodded when she looked at him.

"Good." She turned her back to him and started hunting for skillets. Dalton watched her curves move as she squatted to search the lower cabinets. "How about toast?"

"Sure."

"And will you pour me some coffee?"

She shot him a little grin over her shoulder.

"If you're fixing me breakfast, I can pour you coffee," he agreed and stirred to life. They worked quietly for a moment. Lacy found a bowl to scramble eggs. Dalton poured her coffee and asked if she needed cream or sugar. He found a griddle and laid the bacon on it slab by slab.

Lacy took a long drink of her coffee, set the mug down, and turned to him with knowing eyes.

"Okay, so, I'm not blind. Apparently, Dric is." She shrugged and shook her head. "Here's the thing. Something happened between you and his sister last night, and she wasn't happy about me showing up here this morning."

"No. No, it's not like that—"

"I'm sorry," Lacy said quietly. "I didn't come up here hoping for a weekend of crazy sex with you."

Dalton snorted and tipped his head at her. "Well, now I'm insulted."

He liked her soft and sweet laugh, but not as much as

he liked Journey's loud, hearty laughter.

"I just came out of a bad breakup," she confessed. "Dric and Erin thought they could shove us together and make us have fun. I thought a weekend away...with friends, with some snow and Christmas...stuff...would be good."

Dalton's body melted with relief. He had no desire to whisk this woman off her feet and carry her to bed. No doubt Dric would give him endless grief about wasting opportunities, but it made him feel a hundred percent better that Lacy wasn't interested in him, either.

"Gotcha." He nodded. "But it's not like that with me and Journey."

"Women know, Dalton." She nodded at him. "There was some serious tension in here before she left."

Torn between wanting to hear her thoughts and worry that Dric would overhear them, Dalton stared at her silently.

"You're right that she probably assumed that Dric was trying to set us up," he agreed. "But there's nothing between us. She would have felt uncomfortable being the fifth wheel."

Lacy arched her eyebrows. She held her breath for a moment and finally nodded. "Okay. If that's what you need to tell yourself—"

"Lacy—" Dalton stopped talking and snapped his head around to look toward the door when he heard them on the steps.

"It's okay." She spoke softly. "I'm not gonna tell Dric about what didn't happen and what isn't between you and his sister."

"Did the host say if there're any good hills around for sledding?"

Dalton tore his eyes away from Lacy as Kendric and Erin reappeared in the kitchen doorway. They were holding hands. Dalton wasn't a mushy guy. Well, he could be for the right person, the right woman. Like Journey. But he was no more of a touchy-feely guy than the next. He and Dric didn't have to discuss their friendship to keep it alive. But after the way things had ended with Keely Bartz, Dalton was glad to see that Kendric was finally moving on.

"Sylvia didn't mention it, no," Dalton told him as he grabbed the bread from the end of the counter where he'd left it yesterday. He eyeballed the bacon as Lacy cracked eggs into a bowl. She slipped around him easily, as if they'd been working in a kitchen together forever, to get the milk from the refrigerator.

"You didn't ask?" Kendric sat again at the table.

"Um. No?" Dalton glanced at his friend over his shoulder. "I didn't think to ask. I didn't know sledding was on the agenda. I haven't seen a sled in years."

"I guess we could go scout the area out," he suggested to Erin. Dalton grinded his teeth together to keep his mouth shut. Lacy might be nice, but he didn't want to be thrown with her in forced alone-together times, no matter what Kendric's reasoning might be.

"Let's eat first." Erin rubbed her hands together. She ducked by Dalton to look at the coffee maker. "I can't get warm."

"I'll get it," Dalton told her. She flashed him a smile and watched him select a mug for her. He pushed the thick blue mug to the back of the cabinet, because he had imagined he would give that one to Journey to use. And no matter that Journey had just waltzed out on him and their getaway weekend with her usual smartass smirk, he didn't want anyone else to use the mug he would have given her.

"Thank you." Erin met his eyes as he passed the coffee to her. Panic washed over him, but Erin only smiled and sipped her coffee. If women knew, as Lacy said they did, could Erin tell something had happened between him and Journey? And if she could, would she say something to Dric?

And what about Dric? If he knew Dalton had spent the night in Journey's bed, if he knew Dalton had spent a big part of the night inside Journey's body, would he be pissed? Not like Dric throwing a punch at Dalton would do much but tickle, but Dalton didn't want his friend to be pissed at him. Sisters were off-limits, sure, but Journey wasn't a kid. She was older than he and Kendric, and she wasn't delicate or sensitive. It wasn't like Dalton had seduced her and deflowered her with plans to move on to the next girl today.

His eyes drifted to the woman who would be next if Dric had his way. Erin had wandered back to the table, hands cradled around her mug. Kendric had eyes only for her; he flashed a smile when she sat next to him. Erin slipped her fingers through his. Dalton flashed again to the night before. Teasing Journey about Bryant Abbott. Her thing about guys and lips and her needling him until he admitted that yes, like pretty much every other male on the planet, he liked breasts.

He loved that she hadn't let it go.

Lacy was busy with the eggs, watching the bacon. Not paying attention to him. Because he was stuck with the visual of Journey looking at him skeptically in his SUV yesterday, determined to ignore his question about sleeping with Bryant Abbott, he wanted to talk to her. To Journey. Now. All weekend. What could have been a great weekend was now going to be interminably long and boring, and even worse because he liked the people he was with.

Just not enough.

No one noticed when Dalton slipped out of the room. Mug in hand, he stepped outside to the large, open front porch and wiggled his phone from his pocket. No messages from Journey, no surprise. Though he had expected some sort of parting shot. She hadn't even said goodbye to him. If asked, he would have taken a goodbye kiss. Maybe one more round with her in the shower or in her bed or against her wall, but dammit all, she hadn't even told him goodbye.

If he called her, he would sound clingy. Dalton had learned that early on. The pretty girls might settle for a night with the likes of him, but they didn't want any strings attached. Just because she was Kendric's sister didn't mean Journey would be any different.

Still, he wanted to talk to her. Give her static about just walking out the way she had. Or rib her about Abbott and his red lips. Maybe he should just thank her for dumping him into this weekend as she had. He didn't want to be here now any more than she did.

With a frustrated sigh, he jammed his phone back in his pocket. Better to let it go. Maybe she didn't regret what they had done, but if he tried to keep something going between them now, she might. Best to be a fun memory for her—if she faked orgasms so incredibly good they made her quiver and brought her to tears, she had missed her calling. She could be on Broadway.

"Hey." Dric looked up when he joined them in the kitchen. "Where'd you go?"

Lacy and Erin were setting the table. His stomach growled, and he made a show of checking the breakfast Lacy had prepared. Dalton felt Lacy's stare, but he pretended not to.

"Outside."

"Yeah?" Kendric filled Erin's plate and handed it to her. "Find any hills from your spot on the porch?"

"Actually, it looks like there might be one on the south side of the house."

"Good." Kendric nodded. "We brought the taboggan."

"Thrilling," Dalton mumbled. Before he could keep going, before he rambled that he would rather ride Dric's sister than a taboggan any day, he snatched a piece of bacon from the griddle and tossed it in his mouth.

"So, you're in?" Kendric asked. Dalton loaded his plate and joined the rest of them at the table.

"Sure. Why not?"

"I mean. Unless there's a frozen pond or we make snowmen, there's not a lot to do up here is there?"

Dalton wondered why Dric had been so into the idea of a weekend getaway for the holidays if he felt that way. Then again, ice skating or making snowmen would be fun if you were with the right person.

"What the heck did you and Journey do up here last night?"

Dalton stared at Dric and calmly shoveled a bite of eggs to his mouth. By the time he had swallowed, his heart was no longer beating in his ears and he could breathe well enough he wouldn't sound funny when he spoke.

"I watched TV, and she read."

"What's she reading?"

Dalton wondered why Kendric asked. Surely, he wasn't suspicious, was he?

"Watership Down."

"Oh." Kendric frowned. "I just gave her a stack of books. That wasn't one of them."

"Right. Because who would choose to read that?" Dalton kept his head down. Guilt for attacking anything about Journey weighed him down.

"Right?" Dric laughed. "I gave her some sci-fi stuff."

Dalton's ears perked up. Did Journey like sci-fi? He was curious, but he couldn't ask. Not now. No need to drag this conversation about Journey out. Best to steer her brother away from all things Journey Ryan.

"Which room did you guys pick?" Dalton looked from Dric to Erin. "Tell me not the one next to mine."

"At the end of the hall."

Relieved, Dalton nodded and finished a slice of toast. He didn't want to hear Kendric and Erin any more than he wanted to discuss the things he had done with Journey the night before.

"Is there a room for me?" Lacy asked. "Far away from yours?"

Erin snorted softly. "Plenty."

Dalton ignored the daggers Kendric was shooting at him with his eyes. Nope. He had no intention of inviting Lacy into his room or bed with him.

With a sigh, he sipped his coffee and groaned inwardly at the thought of spending the next two nights here. Without Journey.

9

J ourney went straight home. By the time she pulled Kendric's Jeep into the short drive she shared with the neighboring condo, she had run the gamut of emotions from anger to hurt to relief so many times, her head was pounding. The glare of the sun bouncing off the snow and slicing through the windshield didn't help. At least the roads were clear, and she made good time.

She considered calling Vanessa, but she couldn't bring herself to admit to her best friend that a guy might have bested her. She needed time to process what she had done with Dalton; what had happened had been one hundred percent consensual. But she needed time to think about it. To think about Dalton. The fact that he had willingly crawled into bed with her knowing he would be sharing his bed with someone else tonight. The things he had said to her—on the drive to Kristophe House, over dinner, when he held her after they made love. That he was her brother's best friend, and therefore, technically off-limits.

Even though she was an adult. It wasn't like she was Kendric's little sister, asking Dalton to take her virginity. Hoping to gain a little experience. She wasn't needy or clingy, and she had never gotten attached to anyone she slept with, so it wasn't like Dalton had done something to hurt her.

Hurt like a motherfucker, just the same, she decided as she climbed out of the Jeep, hefted her duffle over her shoulder, and bumped the door closed. The cold air was like icicles in her throat and her chest, so she moved quickly up the drive to her back door. Thankfully, it hadn't snowed much here, so she wasn't looking at shoveling this morning. Although, that would definitely take her mind off Dalton.

Since she had never felt fluttery and downright mopey over a guy, Journey wasn't sure if she was a good liar or not. She had fooled Dric this morning, but then, God love him, Kendric wasn't always good at putting other people first. He wasn't terribly good at reading people, and Journey was good at hiding, so he hadn't stood a chance this morning. Vanessa would see through her though, if she was a bad liar. Better just to hole up alone for the rest of the weekend, do some thinking, and wait a bit before talking to her best friend.

She spared her tree a glance when she walked through the kitchen and down the short hall to her bedroom. If she were feeling festive, she might turn the lights on. But the headache hadn't eased yet, her neck hurt from the drive home, and she hadn't had much sleep last night. Rather than mope, she would sleep instead. She whipped her T-shirt and sweats off quickly, unwilling to go slowly and remember Dalton's gentle touch.

With her condo locked up tight, and her phone on battery fumes, tucked away in her bag, she pulled her comforter back and crawled into bed. Maybe everything would feel different after she slept for a while.

Her bed felt too big. The sheets were too cold. Her skin was itchy and sensitive, and her bra was nearly cutting her in half. She was determined to sleep so she wouldn't have to think about Dalton yet, the way she had explored his body. Her greedy hands smoothing over his hot, slick skin. Her fingers clutching the hard knot of muscle in his upper arms and his shoulders. The flick of her tongue over his nipples—she had laughed when she did it and told him that he definitely tasted better than the last guy she had been with, which had prompted questions like what about the guy before that and before that. Journey had silenced him with her fingers over his lips as she kissed her way down his happy trail.

With a groan, face buried in her pillow, she reached back to unhook her bra and wiggled out of it. Eyes still closed, she tossed it to the floor. The relief was instant and short lived. She could breathe now, but the press of the sheets over her sensitive nipples made her think of Dalton. Dalton with that twinkle in his eyes—Good God, she was thinking in cliches now—as he admitted that he liked breasts and nipples. How he clammed up when she asked how one nipple was different than the next. The way he had scraped his teeth over hers before sucking her hard into his mouth and flattening the tender flesh to the roof of his mouth.

Was he already doing that with the redhead? Were they flirting? Was he using the same lines with the redhead that he had used with her? He couldn't, though.

Because she and Dalton had history. He had started it yesterday in the SUV; he asked her if she slept with Bryant, and he refused to let it go. Journey had gone along with it, thinking he was interested. In her. Not a night of no-strings-attached sex.

Would the redhead ride him with her head thrown back, her hair wild around her as she worked for her own release and delivered his at the same time? Or would she be timid? The idea of the other woman not touching Dalton right, not adding the right amount of pressure when she nibbled on his hip bones before really sinking her teeth in for a hard love bite made Journey's stomach twist with jealousy.

She wasn't going to sleep, and her luck, if she did, she would end up dreaming about Dalton. Not sure she could handle his touch in her dreams, she threw the comforter back and climbed out of bed. Another shower wouldn't hurt. Might ease the tension in her neck. Which might help with the headache.

But she caught her reflection in the mirror as she stepped into her shower. So, naturally, she stopped to study her nude body. And compare it to what she imagined the curvy redhead who was probably at least five years younger than her looked like.

Yep, odds were the other woman looked better naked than she did. She was smoking hot in the skinny jeans and sweater she wore when Journey saw her this morning. She might look better, but Journey doubted she had slept with as many men as she had. Not that it was a bragging point, but on the other hand, Journey knew how to move to please a man.

"Whatever, Journey," she muttered and turned her back on her mirror.

The steamy shower went a long way towards making her feel better. Well, it eased the tension in her neck and whipped the headache. That was good enough. Because Dalton had left some bruises that would take a while to heal.

She had never been big on Christmas movies, but with nothing better to do, Journey pulled on clean yoga pants and a long, loose tunic and curled up on the sofa with a mug of cocoa. She sipped the hot drink, waiting for the comfort it used to bring when her dad made it for her, and focused on a movie about a corporate banker visiting a small town for Christmas.

Hours later, she woke to yet another movie so similar in plot and dialogue, it could have been the same for all she cared. Behind her blinds, daylight was easing into twilight. Her stomach growled, reminding her she hadn't had anything to eat today. The last thing she ate was the soup last night with Dalton.

She turned the tree lights on when she got up and then rummaged in her refrigerator for something to eat. When she found nothing there, she settled for canned soup. Nothing like the homemade stuff last night. But then *tonight* wasn't going to be anything like last night.

Journey took a bowl of soup to the sofa and sank down again to watch TV. She could get dressed and go out. Vanessa wasn't much for clubs or girls' nights in general these days, but Journey had other friends, too. She could call Krystal or April. Hit a bar. Get a drink. Find someone to bring home which would be the best way to get Dalton out of her head.

She pulled her plaid throw over her lap and marveled at the fact that she didn't want to go out. She didn't want to get Dalton out of her head. Or her heart.

———

When the weekend was over and Journey went back to work, Dalton was still in her head. After wallowing all weekend about him, about the things she had done with him, Journey refused to let him take up space rent free in her heart, but damned if she could stop thinking about him. She had even turned into the woman who wouldn't walk away from her phone in case he called or texted her.

And he didn't. Not even once.

At least work was busy. Journey kept her head down and her smile friendly as she directed her employees with weighing and packaging gifts, and during the times business picked up enough that she had to step in and help with customers, she swallowed the knot of emotion and did her job with a smile on her face and true happiness in her voice and her words. Because she did love her job and she did love Christmas—no matter what Dalton believed —and most of her customers these days were shipping Christmas gifts.

Never mind that half the men reminded her of Dalton. And half the women she greeted and helped made her think about the woman her brother had delivered to Dalton for a fun holiday hookup. How was she to know what sort of woman Dalton was into? Maybe he liked curvy redheads. Journey hadn't stuck around to find out, but odds were, Lacy was nice. Kendric considered her a friend, after all.

What bothered Journey most, though, was that Dalton had carried her to her bedroom—after going down on her —and made love to her, spent the entire night in her bed, knowing he would have a different woman to play with the next night. It wasn't so much the fact that he had probably been cozy with Lacy the same night Journey left the bed and breakfast. But that he had so blatantly used her.

Except it *was* the whole other woman thing. Damned if Journey knew what to do with jealousy. Okay, so she might have spent her childhood jealous of the way her mother favored Kendric, but she had never been jealous of another woman having a guy's attention. When it came to her mother, Journey had swallowed it often enough she had internalized the hurt until it was just part of who she was.

Hard to do that with Dalton. She didn't want to internalize that hurt. She kind of wanted to confront him. Give him hell for flat out using her the way he had. But the thought of dragging that night back out to confront Dalton sounded messy. He had hurt her; what if she got emotional with him if she tried to tell him that? She didn't want anything to do with emotions and, God forbid, tears.

"What's going on?" Vanessa nudged her foot under the table. Journey snapped her attention back to her friend. Vanessa tapped her fingers on the stem of her water glass and drilled Journey with a no-nonsense, 'fess up, look.

"Nothing. I'm exhausted." Journey sighed. She glanced around the bar and noted it had gotten busier since she and Van had first come in. Normally, she would love a night like this. Dinner and a drink on a weeknight with her best friend. Paul McCartney's "A Wonderful Christmas Time" piped in for a fun, holiday background sound. People milling about hugging and talking, loud bursts of laughter randomly drowning out everything else.

But instead of enjoying her best friend's time, Journey was still thinking about Dalton. Wondering how his interviews had gone this week. Wondering if he was seeing Lacy now. If they were an item. If at any moment, she might look up and see him walk into Sips with her.

"I'm sure you are," Vanessa agreed. She wrapped her fingers around the stem of the glass. Natural nails. No rings. Vanessa wore only a touch of lip gloss and a swipe or two of mascara. Love, maybe pregnancy, painted her face with radiance and joy. Journey couldn't be happier for her and Parker. Nothing about their relationship had been conventional. Vanessa had propositioned Parker to get her pregnant. Parker—her yard guy—had been taken aback, according to Vanessa, but quick to agree. So quick, in fact, that he had shown up at Vanessa's before they were technically ready to start trying to get pregnant. For a practice run.

Journey had assumed that meant he was eager to jump in the sack with Vanessa and walk away. She had been wrong, though. Love worked for some people. Vanessa and Parker fell in love while insisting that they weren't dating, went at it like bunnies for a while—long enough to get on each other's nerves to the point that they had to take a break. At least the break made Vanessa realize she wanted more from Parker than his sperm. Now they were in the happily-ever-after category, even if it did take them a while to make a baby and even if they weren't in any rush to get to the altar.

"I know you, Journey," Vanessa reminded her. She picked up her glass to sip her water and looked around the bar. "I know something's bothering you."

Journey froze when Vanessa swung her gaze back around to meet her eyes.

"Okay." Vanessa licked her lips. "Tell me why I saw Kendric's Jeep in your driveway last weekend. And lights on in your house. When you were supposedly at Kristophe House."

"Why were you driving by my house?"

"We were looking at Christmas lights," Vanessa mumbled and waved Journey's question away impatiently.

"Oh."

That hit Journey in the heart. Last weekend, she could have imagined going on a date with Dalton. Maybe dinner. Or a movie. Bowling. Maybe dates that involved activity would be a good fit for her and Dalton, since they'd sort of grown up together. A trip to the batting cages in the warmer months. Golf. Vanessa and Parker golfed together.

But after the ride to Kristophe House, the conversation, the night they had spent together, Journey could have imagined a date with him that ended with a drive around to look at Christmas lights. And kissing. And loving.

No. Not loving. Just touching.

The physical act. Nothing more.

"Hey!" Vanessa's eyes widened as she hollered and waved at someone behind Journey. Panicked at the worry that Van might be waving at Dalton, Journey twisted around in her seat to look at the door. Her shoulders collapsed with relief when she saw two women smile and wave back at Vanessa.

"So?" Vanessa turned her attention back to Journey without missing a beat. "Why was Dric's Jeep at your house? Did he not show up at the bed and breakfast?"

Journey would have snorted with sarcasm, but her heart was still in her throat from worry that Dalton might have just walked in. Which was ridiculous. Sips wasn't the only bar in town, and she hadn't seen him in here ever before. She hated being obsessive about this, about him. Odds were, even if Lacy hadn't come to the bed and breakfast with Dric and Erin, even if Journey and Dalton had spent the whole weekend together doing all those dirty things and all the simple things like snowball fights and watching movies together, they wouldn't be dating now. They wouldn't be a couple, because Journey had no interest in being part of a couple.

So, then, why was she sitting here with her head in the clouds, not paying attention to her friend?

"Do you feel okay?"

Journey nodded quickly, although her wine had given her heartburn. "Why?"

"You look really pale suddenly." Vanessa tipped her head to study Journey closely. "Except your cheeks look like they're on fire."

"I'm fine," she mumbled. There was a swallow of wine left in her glass, but she didn't want it. In fact, she wanted to get out of the bar now. Go home. Nurse the broken ego with a cozy blanket and peace and quiet. "Do you mind if we go?"

"No." Concerned now, Vanessa moved quickly.

Journey swallowed her guilt as she watched Vanessa cross to the bar to get their tab. Vanessa had devoured an order of potato skins, all the while giggling and griping about how she was always hungry now. Journey had nibbled on an order of fries and drank most of one glass of wine. Did that mean they were getting old? In the past, the two of them would have killed a bottle of wine and danced until their feet refused to take another step and then taken an Uber home.

Journey zeroed in on Vanessa again. She watched her hand over a credit card to pay the bill and then turn to her right to talk to someone. Still half in a daze, Journey didn't react quickly enough when Vanessa gestured back to her, and suddenly, she and Dalton's gazes locked across the crowded bar.

Her heart—still stuck sideways in her throat—did a major BOOM. Her face flooded with heat. What if he came over to talk to her? What would she say?

But he didn't. That quickly, her heart deflated, and she coughed hard to get it out of her throat and back where it belonged. Stomach on fire now, she arched an eyebrow and tipped her head when Dalton only waved at her, a friendly smile on his face.

As if they were nothing more than the kind of friends you are with your sibling's best friend.

As if they hadn't spent a night as intimately connected as two people could be.

Vanessa reappeared at the table. Journey grabbed her purse and her coat and walked out without a word. How dare he treat her like—like what? The casual hookup she was? The casual hookup she normally preferred to be? Why was this time different?

Once outside, Journey sucked in a breath of cold, sharp air and winced at the sting in her teeth and the knife in her chest. Vanessa was right behind her, bundled up in her coat and gloves. She eyed Journey suspiciously as they walked silently to Vanessa's car.

"You slept with him." Vanessa waited until she started the car and pulled away from the curb before she spoke. And even then, she didn't sound judgmental. Or disappointed.

Still, Journey's heart was somewhere back there on the floor of the bar with strangers walking over it. She wasn't ready to talk about this. Maybe she never would be.

"Did you?"

Christmas music played softly in the car. Journey listened to Mariah Carey crooning away and felt a wave of anger. At herself. One night with her brother's friend had turned her into a girl mooning over a guy, wondering why he couldn't have just walked over to say hello.

When she felt Vanessa's gaze burning into her skin, she simply nodded. Vanessa wasn't the sort of friend to pull out the I-told-you-so. In fact, she only reached over and covered Journey's hand with her own.

Minutes later, they were back at Journey's condo, and Vanessa followed her inside without an invitation. Because they had been friends for so long, Journey left Vanessa in the kitchen while she went on to the bedroom and threw her purse and coat down on the bed. She considered taking her phone out to see if he had at least texted her. But she didn't want to give him the satisfaction. Instead, she kicked out of her skinny jeans and tugged on loose flannel pj pants.

Vanessa appeared in the doorway as she shrugged out

of her blouse and let it fall to the floor. Journey pulled a sweatshirt on, twisted and wiggled out of her bra and let it fall by her blouse, and then turned to her friend.

"That bad?" Vanessa teased.

Journey laughed, but the laugh quickly turned to a sob. She bit her lip to hold the rest in as she perched on the side of her bed.

"Oh boy." Vanessa moseyed into the room and sat beside her.

"That good," Journey whispered when she caught her breath and corralled the emotion inside.

"So, what's—? What happened?"

"It was just sex." Journey cleared her throat. "Incredible sex."

"If it was just sex, you wouldn't be sitting here with glassy eyes, doing your best to hold yourself together."

Journey laughed and dashed at her eyes.

"No. It was just..." She took a steadying breath and shrugged. "I don't know. It felt different."

"Different? Like you feel something for him?"

"No!" Journey insisted. She shook her head and smoothed her hands over her thighs. "No. But. We talked on the drive. He was teasing me about Bryant. And we talked about family and dreams and careers. Life choices."

"And?" Vanessa's soft voice was soothing, but nothing was going to make Journey feel better other than Dalton himself appearing at her front door. And even then, she wasn't sure what he could say to make her feel better.

"Sex with him was different. It wasn't...hard and fast. It wasn't...just a physical thing."

Shoot me now, she thought. She had never said

anything remotely close to those words, and she wished she could open her mouth and take them back now.

"What do you mean?"

Journey stood, frustrated with herself. She knew what she wanted to say, but she couldn't force the words through her lips. Dalton had been *tender* with her. Not gentle. He had touched her with firm, hard hands, and he had driven into her with his hips and thighs, and his hard, giant body had filled her and stretched her. But it had been tender and slow and—

"I slept with him," Journey said on a sigh. "All night. It wasn't a race to get off and get out. I wanted to be with him. To feel his arms around me when we were sleeping."

"You have feelings for him."

"No. I don't," Journey argued. "Other than being fond of him because he's Kendric's friend. I just hate that he used me like that. It's never been that way for me. I've never had a guy complain about no-strings-attached sex. I had no idea it would feel so gross to be used."

"So, you brought Dric's Jeep back early."

Journey rested her butt on the wall and crossed her arms over her chest.

"What happened?"

"I woke up alone. You called. Dalton was downstairs making coffee. And suddenly, Dric was there—"

"I can't imagine Kendric would have an issue with you and Dalton being together."

"Kendric had two girls with him. Erin, of course, and someone for Dalton."

If Vanessa had shrugged the second girl away, maybe Journey could have, too. But Journey was watching her friend closely, so she noticed the tiny wince before Vanessa tried to wipe her face of any emotion.

"But he didn't know when you two went up there early that you would end up together." Vanessa finally found an argument, and Journey had to agree that she was right.

"But. He did know when he took me to bed that Dric was bringing a girl for him to hook up with."

"They're not kids, Journey," Vanessa reminded her. "A weekend away doesn't necessarily mean a big sexfest like it did when we were all younger."

"Except it did," Journey argued. "And no matter if he was supposed to date her or do her, he could have mentioned her to me. Before we did what we did."

"True." Vanessa winced and nodded. She huffed out a sigh as she climbed to her feet. "What did he say about it? About the other woman?"

Journey stared at Vanessa's fingers wrapped around her wrist and finally gave in, letting Vanessa pull her back out to the living area.

"Nothing."

"Nothing?" Vanessa sounded shocked. "That doesn't sound like Dalton. He's not a bad guy, Journey."

"I walked out."

"Do you want more wine?" Vanessa deposited Journey on a stool at the breakfast bar and moved on into the kitchen.

"God, no," Journey groaned. "That wine at the bar gave me heartburn."

"What do you mean you walked out?"

Journey rubbed her eyes and then dragged her hands down over her face. She stared at Vanessa silently.

"Milk?"

"No." Journey turned her nose up. "I'm fine."

Vanessa kicked her shoes off and reached for Journey again. This time she led her into the living room and pulled her down to sit with her on the sofa.

"Tell me."

"Her name's Lacy." Journey dropped her head back to rest on the sofa. "She's pretty. Younger than me."

"Is that what's bothering you?" Vanessa asked softly. "Really? That she's younger than you? That she's pretty?"

Journey closed her eyes for a second and finally rolled her head back and forth on the cushion.

"No."

"You have feelings for him."

"We had a connection, Van. We haven't been around each other much at all in years, but we spent so much time around each other when we were young."

"Feelings," Vanessa whispered.

"And that connection, being so familiar with him made it different. It felt intimate to me in a way sex never has."

"You made love."

"Nope," Journey argued weakly. "I don't do that."

"Just like you don't have feelings for him."

Journey huffed and rubbed her eyes again.

"Doesn't matter. It obviously didn't mean anything to him."

"What did he say when you left, though?"

Journey shrugged. "I dunno. I packed my things, told Kendric I wasn't going to stick around and be the fifth wheel."

"Does Dric know?"

"No!" Journey snapped. "God, no! No. He doesn't need

to know. I wasn't angry. I just didn't want to be in the way."

"Journey, you should have talked to Dalton."

"And say what?"

"You could have told him..."

"What? That one night with him shook me up so much I'm now the stupid girl who checks her phone a hundred times a day to see if he's called? Texted?"

"Are you?"

Journey groaned. "Whatever. It's done. I need to move on."

"Or you could talk to him," Vanessa suggested. "Just sayin.'"

"He didn't seem too eager to come and talk to me tonight, did he?"

"Journey, you're his best friend's sister. You're established—"

"Oh my God, did you just call me old?" Journey pushed up from the couch and paced the living room. She stopped to stare at her tree and realized she hadn't turned the lights on when they came home.

"You've got a reputation for breaking hearts."

"I do not."

"Well, you sure don't have a warm, fuzzy reputation."

"So, now, I'm what? An old—"

"Stop it!" Vanessa climbed to her feet. "Stop. For God's sake, if you can't admit it to me then you're never gonna get what you want here."

"Admit what?" Journey chewed on her lip.

"That you feel something—"

"I don't."

"At least admit to me that you want to see him again. You want to explore things between you and Dalton."

"I'd love to sleep with him again. God, he's incredible—"

"The feelings, Journey. The connection. Not the sex."

10

E ven though Dalton knew the score with Journey, even though he knew what had happened between them at Kristophe House was just a fun hookup between—friends?—he was surprised when she blew him off at the bar. Because even though they had slept together, he did think they were friends. And he had assumed that they would become closer friends, not only because they'd spent the night together. But because they had talked. They'd shared stories; they had talked about his move back home and his reasons why and Journey's situation with her mother.

Seeing her at the bar the other night had been a thrill —the best thing that had happened to him since the night they shared together at the bed and breakfast. Her wave and smile had been a little cool, but it wouldn't have been enough to stop him from going over to talk to her. But by the time he had his beer and passed one off to his buddy, Journey had snuck out.

She didn't even want to talk to him.

That hurt. More than he cared to admit.

Again. Not necessarily because they'd had such an intimate night together, but because he thought above all else, they were friends.

He wanted to catch her up on his job offers. He wanted to tell her he had been offered the position at the memory care facility and the psychiatric ward. That he had accepted the offer from the memory care facility, and that he was looking forward to starting his new journey. Working with the elderly, with dementia patients would surely bring its own bag of challenges, but it felt right to him. Especially now, with his dad ill. Neither of his parents had any memory issues, but it seemed like a good fit. A new challenge, a new experience for him. One that would be rewarding in its own way.

And besides, who knew what the future held? What if one of his parents did eventually exhibit signs of the disease? Dalton wanted to believe someone warm and compassionate would be working with his loved ones in that event. And that belief, that need, had driven him to take the position so that he could be that compassionate person for someone else.

Apparently, it wasn't something Journey wanted to discuss. Apparently, Journey Ryan didn't want to discuss *anything* with him. Not their own aging parents, not her distant relationship with her mother. His job choice. The fact that they'd spent one perfect night together.

At least, Dalton thought it was perfect. Surprisingly intimate and sweet and still, at times, dirty and in his mind, at least, the best sex he had ever had.

When Dalton called to tell Dric about the job offer and his friend suggested dinner and drinks to celebrate,

Dalton worried Lacy would be invited. Sure, he had fun with Lacy after Journey left. As much fun as possible considering it felt like Journey had soaked him from head to toe and then touched a livewire to him and shot a powerful jolt of electricity through him. And then lit a match and threw it on him when she walked out.

Dalton now considered Lacy among his friends, but that didn't mean he wanted to see her. In a date-like atmosphere. They had played a few board games at the bed and breakfast—the four of them—and he and Lacy had binge watched a crime show on TV, and they had bonded over their mutual eye-rolling around Dric and Erin.

But he wanted to see Journey. He wanted to celebrate with Journey. And while Lacy knew the score between them—hell, Lacy had called the score and rules before he ever could—Dric didn't. His buddy was likely to push women at him, not for what he thought would be more casual hookups, but because he knew Dalton would want to find a girl and settle down eventually.

What would Kendric say if he knew Journey was the only woman Dalton was interested in? And not just for her sweet little ass and her hungry kisses?

Didn't matter. Because Journey had no interest in him. Best to get that through his thick head as soon as possible.

Learning the ropes at the memory care facility helped. It kept his mind busy, sure, but Dalton was a nurse, first and foremost, because he genuinely cared about peoples' well-being. He was anxious to learn the new routine and to start caring for his patients.

Within a few days, he would be working twelve hours shifts and be knee deep in other peoples' heartaches, so he wouldn't have time to worry about his own. Kind of pathetic to find himself in such a position before he ever hit thirty years of age, but Dalton was at peace with it. He would rather work away the memory of Journey's soft skin and soft sighs and hearty laughter than chase another woman, other women, to find a fraction of that kind of attraction and fun again.

Kendric, God love him, didn't see it that way.

Dalton sighed and rolled his head on his neck.

"I don't get why it didn't work with Lacy," his friend said now.

"Because there was no chemistry," Dalton mumbled for the fifteenth, maybe sixteenth time.

"She's gorgeous!" Kendric argued. He took another swallow of his beer and plucked a handful of fries from his plate.

"She is," Dalton agreed. "And she's nice. I like her, Dric. But it's not gonna happen."

Kendric stared at him for so long, Dalton worried maybe he was reading his mind. Seeing the night with Journey that continued to play on a loop in his head and his heart. Worried that his friend truly suspected something, Dalton shifted in his side of the booth and leaned forward to prop his elbows on the table.

"I'm just not in a rush," he told Kendric. "Yeah, sure, one of these days, someone like Lacy will be perfect." He looked away from Dric now, because saying that—lying like that to his best friend, lying to himself that he would forget how right it felt to be with Journey that way— killed a little piece of his heart, and Kendric just might notice that. Instead, he looked around the bar, hoping he wouldn't see Journey there.

Hoping he *would* see her there.

"But for now," he swung his gaze back to Kendric, "I need to settle in first. I'm still looking for a place to live. I can't bring a woman back to my parents' house to hang out. Nothing says loser quite like a grown man living with his mom and dad."

Kendric snorted and nodded his agreement.

"And I'm settling in on the job," Dalton continued. "I think it's gonna be a great fit for me. But it's exhausting."

"It will be a great fit for you man," Kendric agreed. "But it will be exhausting and time-consuming. I don't wanna see you get towed under and not come up for air for the next three years. Only to find everyone's passed you by."

Dalton considered Kendric's worry. It just didn't matter so much to him. If he couldn't have the chance to get to know Journey better, to see if they had more than one night together, getting left behind while his buddies started their families didn't really matter to him.

"No hurry here, Dric," he said quietly.

Kendric nodded. He set his bottle down and shot a hand through his hair. "I was thinking about asking Erin to move in with me."

Dalton snapped his attention back to Kendric.

"Yeah?"

Kendric only nodded.

"She's pretty great."

"She is," Kendric said with a grin. "We've been together seventeen months. It just feels like it's time."

Dalton tipped his head. "Like on some big timeline? Of relationships?"

"No, man." Kenric blew out a sigh. "I don't think there

is such a thing. No guidelines. If you don't feel it, it's not gonna work just because you followed a formula or a rule book."

"And yet you're pushing me and citing a timeline."

Kendric's grin this time was a bit sheepish.

"Maybe Erin and I want someone to double date with."

Dalton laughed as if the idea of double dating was ridiculous and old-fashioned, when really he loved the sound of it. Dric and Erin and him and Journey. Out for dinner. Dancing. Cooking out.

"I'm content to be the third wheel for a while." Dalton pushed his empty longneck away.

"I think she's the one."

Dalton caught himself before he could respond. Before he could blurt out that damned right, Journey was the one.

"Erin?"

"Who else?" Kendric shrugged. "You want another one?"

"Nope. I'm good."

"So, I was gonna run it by Journey first. What do you think?"

Dalton was suddenly glad for the poor lighting in the rinky-dink tavern they had chosen for burgers and fries, because he was pretty certain the color had just drained from his face. He had been so careful not to bring Journey up, when all he wanted to do was talk about her. But he knew that would be a dangerous game, so he forced himself to swallow her name every time he felt her there on the tip of his tongue.

Uncomfortable now, thinking about the parts of her

body where his tongue had been as he looked her brother in the eyes, Dalton shifted again in the booth.

"Run what by her?"

"Asking Erin to move in."

Dalton considered asking Dric why he needed Journey's approval. Kendric was an adult, the same as he was. He might have been a little spoiled by his mother and sister, too, but the guy was standing on his own two feet now. He had a degree in engineering and a decent entry level job at a firm here in town. Not to mention that Journey was soured on any sort of intimate relationship between the opposite sexes. Why would her opinion matter to Kendric?

And yet, Dalton knew Kendric and Journey were close. So yes, her opinion, her guidance, still mattered very much to Kendric.

"Sure." Dalton shrugged. He wasn't sure it was a good idea, though. What if Dric trotted the idea by her and she vetoed it? Reminded him of how things had ended with Keely? Gave him a lecture on how romance was fleeting and commitment nearly impossible?

She might encourage Dric to dump Erin and move on. The depressing thought was enough to give Dalton a headache.

11

Christmas would be the same this year, and that fact made her angry. Kind of made her sad, which only fueled her anger. Never in a million years did Journey believe she would have a meaningful night with someone, so having had the experience and finding herself alone and unchanged on the other side of that night pissed her off. She had given herself—heart and all—to someone without realizing she had done it, and now she was alone and moping, and Christmas was just around the corner, and she would be handling the holiday season and family obligations alone. Just like always.

She shoved the vacuum cleaner back into the closet and retraced her steps back to the kitchen. Four o'clock on a Saturday afternoon usually found her with plans to go out for a drink, most often with a girlfriend, although not Vanessa these days, not since she found Parker. Today, Journey had no plans to go anywhere other than her living room sofa. She had worked until after seven every night this past week. The extended holiday hours usually invigorated her and made her happy, more festive. But she had come home every night this week drained. This morning, she had climbed out of bed at six to be at work by seven, and of course, the Saturday before Christmas was insanely busy. The only good thing about working her butt off today had been not wondering what Dalton was up to, if he had plans for this weekend.

She wondered that the second she climbed into her car to come home, though, so as soon as she walked into the house, she kicked off her shoes and started cleaning. Even though she lived alone and had just cleaned the condo earlier in the week.

Now she took a quick shower, dressed in skinny jeans and a white button up blouse, and added a dab of lip gloss and a stroke of mascara to her lashes. Determined to do something, to get out of the house even if it meant going to hang out at Vanessa's and be a third wheel, she went to her closet in search of shoes. Standing in the doorway, she studied her collection, torn between navy flats, her gray-heeled boots, and her warm, cozy slippers. Because if she were honest with herself, she really had no desire to go out. Certainly not alone, which made her angry, because she used to do it all the time.

The ring of the doorbell shot a little dose of calm chasing through her veins. She hadn't wanted to tell Vanessa about Dalton, but now she was glad that she had. They had talked that first night about it. And Vanessa had reminded Journey a few times that she was a good listener if she wanted to talk. Journey didn't, because talking to Vanessa wouldn't change anything, but at least her friend wasn't nagging her about it.

Journey, still barefoot, went back down the hall to

answer the door. She wondered where Parker was tonight, but then again, if Vanessa was here to hang out with her, Journey wasn't going to question her friend. Journey had seen enough to know Parker and Vanessa were the real deal, and the thought of binge-watching TV over a shared bowl of popcorn with her best friend made her happy.

Her heart, her stomach, crashed when she pulled her door open to find Dalton on the small porch, hand raised as if ready to ring the bell again.

"Dalton."

Good grief, did her voice sound all breathy and nervous? What the hell was wrong with her? Why did this guy have this power over her?

"Hey." He jammed his hands into his hip pockets and arched his eyebrows.

"What're you doing here?"

This time, she was relieved to sound a bit harsh. Good. She didn't want him here.

Well, she did, but damned if she would admit that to him.

"Can I come in?"

Rather than blurt out what she was thinking—*Why? What do you want?*—Journey stepped back to give him space to come inside. Even if this was a short conversation in which she told him off, it was freezing standing there with the door open.

"What do you want?"

The words were out before she could stop them, but remembering the night they shared, remembering the next morning, she decided she didn't care if she sounded blasé or aggressive. She dragged her eyes away from him, though, when he appeared to be sizing her up. Dammit. Didn't do her much good to sound tough if she was going to shrink away from making eye contact with him.

"I wanted to talk to you about Kendric," he finally told her.

"What about Kendric?" She tipped her head and narrowed her eyes at him. "Oh, damn. You didn't tell him, did you?"

When he didn't answer her right away, Journey's heart did a giant harsh BOOM and then took off at a gallop. Was Kendric upset about what had happened? Surely, it wasn't that big of a deal, was it?

But why in the hell had Dalton even told him?

"Jesus, Dalton, you told him we slept together?" She wiped her damp palms over her denim-clad hips and tried her hardest to keep her eyes off of his.

"No!" As if stung by her accusation, Dalton finally snapped. He turned away from her and paced across the living room. She watched from where she stood, hating that she liked the site of him standing by her Christmas tree.

"Then how does he know?"

"He doesn't know!" Dalton threw his hands up in frustration.

"Then what're you doing here? Why do you need to talk to me about Dric?"

When he didn't answer her immediately, Journey walked out of the room. In the kitchen, she pulled a tall boy from her refrigerator and popped the top. Dalton followed her a second later. Rather than offer him a beer, Journey took a swig and started at him boldly.

"What? Just tell me."

"Why would it be a big deal if he knew?" Dalton spoke quietly now. His frown confused her. Was he angry that she didn't want her brother to know they slept together? Maybe if Dric questioned either of them outright, she would understand Dalton's desire to tell the truth. But why bring it up if Kendric had no idea?

"What?" She took a long drink and set the can on the counter. "Are you here because you want to tell him? Is it guilt? Do you feel like you have to apologize for what we did?"

"No." He took a step toward her. Journey moved, backed into the counter with her hips. "But I wanna know why it matters. Are you embarrassed? That we slept together?"

The words took her breath away. Looking into Dalton's eyes when he said them was almost more intimate than the things they had done together that night.

"I'm a big girl, Dalton. I do what I want." She shrugged, pretending a nonchalance she didn't feel. "Kendric doesn't need to know who I sleep with."

"Have there been others?" Dalton stood so close his voice rumbled in her chest. "Since we were together?"

Journey blinked, shocked that he had the nerve to ask her that.

"What?"

He lifted his hand and stroked his fingers over her cheekbone.

"Don't." She tried to block him. The tenderness in his fleeting touch when she missed made her heart hurt.

"I miss you."

Now he sounded sweet, almost playful, and the change

in the air—the *charge* in the air—between them stole her breath away again.

"No, you don't."

"Journey."

"Dalton, don't." She shook her head when he leaned down to kiss her, but her body moved without her permission. She pushed up on her tiptoes and tilted her head back so his lips could brush hers. That first press of his warm mouth to hers rendered her dizzy, and she grabbed his upper arms to hold on.

"Don't?" he repeated.

"No." She shook her head, uncertain now if she meant don't kiss her or no, never mind that she had said no. Their faces so close she could feel his breath on her lips, she waited. He kissed her again, and this time he added a soft kiss on the corner of her mouth and then nipped at her chin. Somehow his fingers were on her neck. Could he feel her pulse racing there?

"Dalton." She shook her head.

"We need to talk about this," he told her, his voice firm and unyielding as if he had suggested it before and she had said no.

"We don't, though," she argued. "We don't need to talk about it. Ever."

"Then why are you kissing me back? If you don't want to talk about it? About us?"

With her eyes closed, the sudden onslaught of tears had nowhere to go. Journey held her breath for a second. Dalton's hands slid down her sides to her hips; his parted lips now on hers again. The feel of his hard, warm body so close sent her back to the bed and breakfast, when she had found safety in his arms.

A red flag waved in her mind. There might not be rules against this since she was an independent woman, but kissing him like this was only going to bring more heartache. Her hands ignored the red flag though, and she gripped his muscled arms tighter when he stroked his tongue over hers.

"What the hell is going on here?"

Too out of breath and too into Dalton to move, she ducked her head when she heard her brother's voice.

"Dric." Dalton croaked the name out.

"What the hell are you doing with your mouth on my sister?"

Furious heat rushed to Journey's cheeks, but with her forehead pressed to Dalton's chest now, Kendric wouldn't notice.

"Kendric, this is—"

"Seriously?" Dric groaned. "Oh my god. *This? This* is why you weren't interested in Lacy? Because you have a thing for—"

Journey turned her face to look at Kendric. His jacket was unzipped, as if he was yanking it off when he strolled into her house unannounced, expecting to talk to her and instead finding her making out with his friend.

"You slept with her." Kendric's eyes jumped from Journey up to meet Dalton's gaze. "You banged my sister the night you were at the bed and breakfast?"

Journey cringed. "Dric."

"You son-of-a-bitch." Kendric drew back as if Dalton had taken a swing at him.

"Dric, can you give us a minute?" Journey's voice came out as a whisper.

"What the hell, man? You don't fuck around with your friend's sister. That's not cool. That's not code—"

"For God's sake, Dric, grow up!" Journey snapped. "There's no code. And this isn't your business."

"You're gonna let her defend you? Speak for you?" Dric asked Dalton.

"Can you please give us a minute, Kendric?" Journey pulled away from Dalton. She folded her arms over her chest, thankful things hadn't progressed any further than a long, tender kiss. Chin tucked to her chest, she turned her back on both of them and paced across the room.

"Sure, Journey." Kendric sounded pissed, but at the moment, he was the least of her concern. Right now, her worry over what Kendric was thinking took a back seat to her fury with Dalton for using her, for waltzing in here and kissing her now after two weeks of ignoring her. "Sure. You call me when you're ready to tell me what the hell you're doing with Dalton McKenzie."

With her back to Dalton, she listened until she heard the front door close behind Dric before she dropped her arms and took a deep breath.

"Is he okay?" Journey cleared her throat and tossed her head back to wait for Dalton's response.

"You're really more worried about what he thinks than what's going on between us?"

Journey turned to Dalton with a frown and waved his words away.

"You came over her to talk to me about him, and then he showed up. Is he okay?"

"He's fine." Dalton nodded. "He's thinking about asking Erin to move in with him. And he wants your opinion. Your blessing." Dalton shook his head and shrugged. "I don't know."

Journey watched him scrub his hand over his buzzcut hair and then squeeze the back of his neck.

"And?" she asked with an overly dramatic shrug of her shoulders.

"I was afraid you would try to talk him out of it."

Journey blinked, confused with the direction their conversation had taken.

"Why would I do that?"

"Because you're not into relationships. And that's fine for you, but Kendric's in love with her. I think Erin might be the one."

Journey took a deep breath and tipped her head to study Dalton.

"So, you think that I want my little brother to be alone and miserable just because—" she caught herself before she could finish her sentence. *Just because I am.* She had almost said that out loud to Dalton. The guy who made her stop and feel.

And wonder.

Was she alone and miserable? Had she been lying to herself all along? Or had Dalton just made her stop and wonder if she wanted to be alone the rest of her life? And now that she was caught up in that drama, she was unhappy. Miserable seemed a bit strong for her emotions, but unhappy certainly fit.

Maybe a *little bit miserable* that Dalton had blown her off after the night they shared together.

"Do you?"

"No, Dalton. I don't," she answered simply.

"Okay, so let—"

"I think you should go."

Hurt that Dalton would believe that about her, that she would want someone she loved to be alone just because she was, Journey couldn't wait to boot him out the door. To be alone. Again. Maybe she was better off with the devil she knew.

"I don't think we're done talking."

With a long, drawn-out sigh, Journey met his eyes and arched her eyebrows.

"I don't think there's anything to say."

"I didn't sleep with Lacy."

Damn it all, if those words didn't needle her heart, poking hard enough to puncture and slip inside.

"I'm not doing this, Dalton." She shook her head.

"Why did you just walk out?"

She eyed him silently for a moment. He wasn't going to leave until they had it out. When she'd walked out of Kristophe House the morning after they slept together, she had been hurt and confused. Now she simply regretted what they had done. Dalton had hurt her, and now he seemed determined to hammer away at what was left of their friendship.

"Seriously?"

"You went from wanting to shower with me to packing your bag and storming out within ten minutes."

"I didn't storm out," she corrected him. Already impatient with his excuses, with the whole situation, Journey folded her arms over her chest.

"True." He nodded. "And that's it in a nutshell. Right?"

"What?"

"Girls like you—"

"Whoa, whoa, whoa." Journey shook her head and

flashed him the palm of her hand. "What does that mean? *Girls like me?*"

"Journey—"

"It was a hookup, Dalton. I get it." Exhausted now, Journey dropped to sit at her two-top table. "Obviously, *girls like me* get that. But you could have said something. You could have told me Dric was bringing you..." She bit her lip and reminded herself Lacy was probably a nice person and didn't deserve for Journey to rip on her. "That he was hoping to set you up with Erin's friend. And even after what we did, you could have talked to me. You could have called me to make sure I got home okay. You could have talked to me at the bar the other night, instead of blowing me off."

"I blew you off?" His loud bark of laughter pounded her between the eyes. "I waited for my beer and turned around to come and talk to you, only to see you haulin' ass outta there."

"Okay. Then let's call it even." She shrugged. "*Girls like me* don't get caught up in drama like this—"

"You're pretty, Journey."

Dalton's seemingly out-of-nowhere announcement made her head spin.

"What?"

"*Girls like you.*" He pulled the other chair out to sit across the table from her. "*Pretty girls like you* don't take guys like me seriously. They never have. Never will." He shrugged.

"Guys like you? What? What're you talking about?"

"Girls like you, pretty, independent girls like you don't fall for guys like me."

Journey groaned and covered her face with her hands.

"I'm the fun guy. I'm always just the friend. Maybe the friend who gets a girl over a breakup with some laughs and miniature golf or a movie. I'm the big guy who tags along with a couple of girls on a night out to make sure nobody drugs them. I'm the protector. I'm good with that. But none of those girls ever really wants to be with me."

"So, after *using* me at the bed and breakfast, instead of at least being my friend, you just totally blew me off. Before I could do the same to you? Is that what you're saying?"

"I didn't *use* you at the bed and breakfast," he argued quietly. "That night..." He cleared his throat. "I wanted that night to be the beginning of something."

Journey dropped her hands to the table to stare at him. That night had definitely felt like the beginning of something, but she had decided she imagined it when Kendric had shown up at Kristophe House with Erin and her friend Lacy the next morning.

"I have no doubt you're gonna fall for someone, Journey. You're tough, and you're independent, but after the night we shared? Seeing that soft, vulnerable side that you never share with anyone? I know you'll fall." Dalton cleared his throat. "But I know it won't be for me."

"And that excuses you being an ass to me since we were together?"

"I'm sorry." He held her gaze. The hell of it was, he sounded sincere. "I should have called. I should have asked you to stay that weekend."

"I couldn't stay there," she argued. "I didn't want to watch you play out the same damned things with her that you did with me the night before."

"I didn't know Kendric was bringing Lacy. And I

promise you nothing happened with her. We watched some crime show. The four of us played some board games. And the rest of the weekend sucked, because I just wanted to be with you."

Journey sucked in a sharp breath, but her chest was tight with pent up emotion, and it hurt to breathe.

"Dammit, Dalton." She pressed the heels of her hands into her eyes and groaned. "I don't know how to do this."

"Do what?"

Journey lowered her hands to the table and chewed on her lip. Afraid to meet his eyes, she stared at her hands and wondered what a ring would look like on her third finger. A diamond ring. She hadn't ever thought she was that kind of girl, and the idea that she maybe she was scared the hell out of her.

"I don't know how it feels," she licked her lips, "but maybe I am falling. Maybe I *want* to fall."

"Journey?"

When he tipped his head, she flicked her eyes up to meet his.

"For you," she whispered. She pulled her hands back when he reached over the table to touch her. "I don't know what the hell this is, but you're all I can think about."

"Me, too."

Journey swallowed hard and took a deep breath. "What do we do now?"

"Right now." He turned his hand over on the table and arched his eyebrows. "Right now, I really want to kiss you again."

Reluctantly, she reached out and touched his fingers.

"I want you to kiss me."

"C'mere."

On weak knees, Journey climbed from her chair and rounded the table. Dalton reached for her and settled his hands on her hips. Eyes locked with his, she let him pull her into his lap.

"I didn't mean to hurt you." His lips brushed hers.

"I didn't mean to fall for you." She tipped her lips up in a quick smile; but hungry for more of him, for his affection, she kissed him again. "I didn't plan to ever do this, but there's something about you, Dalton."

"Something about us," he corrected her. Journey felt his arms tighten around her.

"What if this doesn't work?" She smoothed her fingers over his face and linked her hands behind his neck.

"But what if it does?"

"What about Kendric?"

"Maybe we can worry about Kendric later?"

"He was pretty pissed," she reminded him with a soft laugh. "I don't want to come between you guys."

"I don't wanna lose a friendship, but I won't lose you, Journey. Not again."

Journey nibbled a path from his lips to his ear and then sank her teeth into his earlobe.

"Did you have plans for tonight? You look like you were going out."

She drew back to look him in the eye again. "I was planning to go out and drink."

"Alone?"

She rolled her lips inward and nodded. "If that's what it was going to take, yes."

"Would you have come home alone?"

"I don't want anyone else." Her voice was husky and thick with desire. "Not after being with you."

Journey pressed her thumb to his lip and dragged her eyes over his face before looking him in the eyes again.

"We could still go out," he suggested.

"Or we could just stay in," she said hopefully.

Journey still in his arms, Dalton stood to carry her away from the table. Journey locked her ankles around his waist and held on as she directed him to her bedroom.

12

B eing with Journey today was a bit more like what Dalton expected to begin with. Once inside her bedroom, Journey let go of him for a second to swing her door shut. That had slowed him down, because even as she wiggled against him to get out of her blouse and bra, Dalton remembered Kendric had just shown up and let himself into her house earlier. What if he did it again? Dalton didn't plan to hide what was going on between himself and Journey, not anymore. But he didn't really want Kendric to see it, either. Not up close and explicit.

But Journey's bare breasts pressed up against him as she sampled ticklish spots on his neck with her teeth shoved Kendric to the back burner again. Dalton painted his hands over the soft skin of her back and slid his fingers into the waistband of her jeans, craving those throaty moans of pleasure she made weeks ago, that he still hadn't forgotten.

Ass cheeks cupped in his palms, Journey drew back to look him in the eyes.

"Not yet," she whispered.

"No?" Surprised that she was pumping the brakes, he waited for her to explain.

Journey released her legs and shimmied down his body. Dalton gritted his teeth as she slid over his rock-hard dick and prayed for mercy. She wouldn't flash him her breasts and then change her mind so quickly, would she?

"This." She reached for his hands, now hanging limply at his sides. Dalton watched her place them on her breasts, her hands cupping his. "Touch me here."

"When this is over." Dalton stroked his thumbs around the curves of her breasts. "If we make love—"

"I want you to make love to me," she interrupted with a whisper.

"But when I get out of your bed." He dragged his gaze from hers down over her bare shoulders and watched her hands move over his as he caressed her. "Is this real? This time?"

He tipped his chin in time to see the flash of pain in her eyes. She sank her front teeth into her lip, and Dalton felt a kick of lust explode in his groin. He wanted those full lips on him. On his chest. His belly. His cock.

"I wanted last time to be real, Dalton." She stepped closer to him and lifted her hand to cup his face. "I don't know. Maybe I'm doing this all wrong, because I've never wanted to do it right."

Blood raged through his body again when he gently pinched her nipple and her eyes glazed with lust.

"I want to," she whispered. "I want to do this. With you."

"Journey."

"I want it to be real."

Dalton stood still when she skimmed her fingers down his sides to gather his shirt tail in her hands. He liked the weight of her breasts in his hands, but he wanted to lay her down on her bed and kiss her. To taste her breasts and sample the dark centers with his tongue and his teeth. Quickly, he let go of her and took over with his shirt. He whipped it over his head quickly and let it fall to the floor at their feet.

When he reached for her, Journey climbed him like a tree, her knees pressed firmly around his waist, her fingers wrapped around the back of his head. She straightened in his arms to give him access to her breasts, and Dalton obliged, flicking first one nipple with his tongue and then the other. They moved in a frenzy, scrambling up over the end of the bed, and then she lay before him. Eyes locked with his, Journey opened her legs and tugged him firmly into place between her thighs.

"Kiss me." The command was clear, her voice just short of desperate.

He kissed her. Everywhere. Even after he had eased her jeans and panties down over her legs, teasing her with feather light kisses on her thighs and her knees, and even after he tasted her core again and drove her on a wild ride to orgasm, he kissed her again and again.

Finally, with strength that surprised him, Journey—still breathing hard from the orgasm—gave him a shove and flipped him over to lie on his back. Her mouth on his, her teeth on his tongue, Dalton felt her fingers work his jeans open. He lifted his hips as she scooted back over him and tugged them down just enough to free his cock.

"No way." He laughed and reached for her, but she dodged his hand.

"Tell me you have condoms." She lifted her gaze to his and arched an eyebrow as a warning.

"In my wallet."

Dalton, so turned on his dick might break, watched her snatch the leather bifold from his back pocket and then pluck three condoms from it.

"Damn," she groaned. "I'm gonna assume you're just always prepared and not complain since I get the benefits."

"Journey." He grabbed fast and wrapped his fingers around her wrist. Stunned, she stared at him with wide eyes, the condoms still in her hand. "I haven't been with anyone since that night we were together. I put the condoms in my wallet today on the one chance in hell I had of being with you again."

"I haven't, either," she whispered as she climbed back up his body to kiss his lips. "I promise, Dalton, I haven't been with anyone since you."

Her kiss was slow and tender, like a promise, but hot and searching. Dalton eased his hard grip on her wrist and moved to touch her again.

"No." She pulled away from his mouth to argue. "I need you inside me."

He took the condoms from her, dropped two and yanked one open. Journey watched him roll it on. Before he could move, before he could try to kick out of his jeans, she lowered herself over him and took him in as deep as she could.

"Journey."

"Let me." She rocked over him, eyes locked with his again. "Let me do it."

This was the woman he had imagined her to be before he took her to bed at the bed and breakfast. She rode him hard and fast, her hands exploring her own body for his viewing pleasure. Dalton fought to control himself, wanting to make it last. Wanting to make her come before giving into his own need for release. She came hard, her body rigid over his, one hand splayed on his belly and the other arm bent behind her head and her fingers tangled in her hair. Desperate to follow her, Dalton arched his back, cupped his hands over her hips to hold onto her, and pumped his hips up high and hard, shouting her name as the orgasm ripped through his body.

Spent, Journey cut loose with a long growl and moan and draped herself over him.

"Did she try to seduce you?"

"Hmm?"

Dalton frowned and rolled his head on the pillow to look at Journey. Lying over him, she smoothed her fingers over his lips and kissed his cheek.

"Erin's friend."

"No."

"Don't lie." She shook her head the slightest bit and pressed her lips together. "Please, just always be honest with me."

"She didn't," he told her. "She knew immediately that something had happened between us. And she said she was just off a bad breakup and just wanted some time away."

"You just told me you're the guy to get a girl over a bad breakup."

"Journey." He took her hand in his and kissed her fingers.

"She's younger than me."

"But she's not you," he argued.

"Are you sure about this?"

Dalton's heart boomed and hammered painfully in his chest.

"You're not?"

"I'm a handful, Dalton," she said simply. "I've got more baggage than a 747. Most guys wouldn't want to deal with that."

"Do you remember when I came home from school the first time? You were dating that Jack guy?"

She snorted softly and nodded.

"I hated that dick," he told her.

"Why?" Her lips tipped up in a slow, lazy grin. She eased over to lay at his side. Dalton sighed with content when she slid her toes down his leg and rested her hand on his belly.

"Because I overheard him talking about having sex with you in the bathroom of some bar."

"Oh." Journey winced. "I'm sorry."

"I wanted to throat punch him for talking about you that way."

"It's who I am," she reminded him. "That's why you need to be sure you can be with me."

"I will have sex with you anywhere you want me. I'll treat you to champagne and roses and silk sheets, and I'll make love to you seven ways from Sunday every damned day. And I'll be filthy dirty and get down on my knees for you in any bar bathroom you want."

"Dalton." Journey scraped her teeth over her lip.

"Just be with me, Journey. Just me."

She traced a path from his belly button up over his chest and finally she touched his lips again.

"You did something to me." Her whisper was thick with longing.

"I love doing things to you."

Dalton loved the grin that crept over her face, but even more, he was in love with the blush in her cheeks.

"I don't even mean that, Dalton." She met his eyes. "Talking to you that night. Before we made love. It was like you saw me."

"I've always seen you, Journey."

Dalton lifted his head from the pillow to kiss her.

"How?" She spoke against his lips.

"What?"

"How did you see me? You were just a kid."

"I don't know." He pushed his fingers back through her hair. "But I have. I think I've been a little bit in love with you since I was that kid."

"Don't." She tipped her head down to rest on his shoulder.

"No?"

"Not yet."

"Okay." He smoothed his hand down over her back. "Who's gonna tell Kendric?"

The laughter that rumbled up through her belly and tumbled from her lips thrilled him.

"I will." She snuggled closer to lick his neck. "He won't be tempted to hit me."

"You think he's gonna do any damage if he takes a swing at me?"

Journey lifted her head to peek at him. "To himself, maybe?"

Dalton chuckled.

"Seriously. Can I talk to him first?" she asked softly.

"We could talk to him together," Dalton suggested.

"I'm afraid that might just make him angrier."

"Okay." He sighed. "I meant it, Journey. I don't want this to come between me and Dric, but I don't want to let you go."

"I'm not going anywhere," she promised. "Oh God!" She laughed and groaned. "What have you done to me? Pining away over you. Wishing you would call me. Making you promises."

"Maybe you just finally saw how special I am." He grinned and dragged his hand up over her back and threaded his fingers through her hair again.

"Maybe I did." She nodded. "Will you kiss me again?"

"Where?" He arched his brows as she slid over on top of him.

"Mmm." She grinned. "I like that idea, but I meant like this." Framing his face in her hands, she took his mouth in a slow, wet kiss. "I used to hate kissing like this."

"And now?" He rubbed his lips over hers.

"Must be you." She nipped at his lower lip and caught it in her teeth. "I love my mouth on yours."

"I love—"

"Dalton."

"Being here with you."

She laughed softly and kissed him again. "There's one other thing."

"What?"

"What about Christmas?"

"Is that an invite? To spend the holidays with you?"

"Would you?"

"I would love to." Dalton flipped her over and pressed her into the mattress. "You sure you want your parents to know about us? What will Lenore say?"

"I don't care." Journey shifted and parted her legs again so he could settle between them. "Vanessa knows about us."

"You told her?"

"Yep. The night you blew me off at Sips."

"Journey—"

She grinned. "I'm teasing. Dalton?"

"Hmm?" He leaned in to kiss her neck and nibbled up to her ear when she turned her head to give him more room.

"Again?" she whispered. "Make love to me? Again?"

13

Journey stomped her feet on the tiny front porch at her brother's apartment, hoping to get some blood circulating to warm her toes before they fell off. She pounded on the door again and hunched deeper into her wool coat while she waited for Dric to open the door.

When he did, he turned and walked back into his small living room without a word to her. Journey sucked in a deep breath to summon some patience and stepped inside. Maybe she should have let Dalton take the lead on this.

She considered texting Dalton as she followed Dric to his small galley kitchen, but she didn't. After all, she'd just said goodbye to him a few hours ago when he climbed out of her bed to go home and shower before going to work. When she mumbled a question about working on Sundays, he kissed her cheek and told her it wasn't an every-Sunday thing and that he would call her later.

"Can I have some?" she asked when Dric poured himself a cup of coffee.

He sighed and gestured at the coffeemaker as he sank back to lean on the counter and took a drink of his own. At home in his apartment, Journey helped herself to a cup and then rested on the counter opposite him and stared him down.

"Are you seriously pissed about this?"

"Wouldn't you be?" He refused to give in, his tone still gruff with anger.

"Kendric—"

"How would you feel if you walked in on me all over Vanessa?"

Journey opened her mouth to answer him, but she realized she wasn't sure how she would feel about it and gritted her teeth.

"I had no idea he would hit on you that weekend," Kendric continued before Journey could sort her thoughts to answer him. "If I had been there, nothing would have—"

"Kendric." Journey sighed. "It wasn't like that."

"He didn't take advantage—"

"No." She sipped from her coffee and rubbed her eyes with her free hand. "First of all, I'm not a kid. He didn't steal my virginity. He didn't force himself on me."

"I don't want to talk about your virginity, Journey."

"Good, because I lost it when you were still in middle school."

"You're missing my point." Kendric groaned and turned his back to her.

"I'm not," she said softly. "We were both flirting. Both into it. Don't blame him."

"So, here's something, Journey." Dric crashed his coffee mug down on the counter. "Two days ago, Erin and I had a pregnancy scare. And here I am, can't talk to my best friend about it because he's banging my sister."

Journey bit her lip. "She's not pregnant?"

"No."

Was it her imagination, or did Kendric sound disappointed?

"Did you want her to be?"

"What I want is to erase the last month and change things."

"Dric, I want to be with him," she whispered.

Kendric groaned and muttered something long-winded that sounded mean-spirited.

"Was that the first time? That weekend?"

"Yes," she said firmly. When Kendric gave her a suspicious look, she nodded to assure him. "We didn't go into that weekend thinking about it. It just—it happened."

"Would you have told me if I hadn't walked in on you yesterday?"

Her hesitation threw Kendric into a fit of anger again. Journey watched him stalk around the tiny kitchen, flinging the dishtowel to the opposite end of the counter and opening and closing a cabinet with a bang.

"I don't know how to answer that, because before you walked in on us yesterday, I hadn't talked to him since I left the bed and breakfast."

"But you want to be with him."

Hard to miss the sarcasm in his voice.

"Being with him was..." She cleared her throat and looked away from Kendric's hard stare. "Different, Kendric. It felt...familiar. It felt right."

"So right that you didn't talk to him for two weeks." He nodded.

"Well, you showing up with an extra for Dalton the next morning kind of threw a wrench in things."

"Damn." Kendric dropped his head back and groaned again. "I'm sorry. I just had no idea something like that would happen with you two."

"I didn't, either, Dric," she insisted. "But I want you to know I walked into it eyes wide open. I wanted—just don't blame him."

"He didn't sleep with her," Kendric told her. He picked up his coffee and propped his hip on the counter again. "He had no interest in Lacy. I thought he was crazy."

"Well, I was crushed when you walked in with her." Journey shrugged. "And I had no idea what to do with that feeling."

"So." Kendric stared at a spot on the floor. He took a quick peek at her, but he didn't hold the eye contact. "Yesterday? Did you guys—"

"We talked," she answered simply.

"Long talk." Kendric made a show of looking at his watch.

"Do you want details?"

"Nope." He shook his head. "No, I do not want details."

"Are you okay with this?" she asked after a few moments of silence. "Because we want to be together. We both want to..." She shrugged and shook her head, still shell-shocked to realize she had feelings for Dalton. "Give this a chance."

Kendric answered with a deep, dramatic shrug. "Guess I have to be, don't I?"

"Please be okay with it, Dric. I don't wanna come

between you guys, but I don't wanna give up something that feels so right."

"I never thought I'd see the day or the guy who would tame Journey Ryan," Kendric mumbled. He put his cup down again and smashed the heels of his hands into his eyes. "I can't get the image of you and Dalton kissing out of my head."

"Maybe you should knock next time."

"Trust me." He nodded and dropped his hands to his sides. "I will."

"What about Erin?"

"What about her?"

"Is she okay? Did you guys want a baby?"

Kendric hesitated, but he finally gave Journey a quick shrug. "I mean, no. Not yet. But you know, you have that short time frame when you think it might be happening, and you kind of get your hopes up."

"I don't know," she whispered. "About babies. But I do know what it feels like to hope for something."

Their eyes met.

"Dalton gave me that, Dric."

"I'm in love with her," Kendric told her. "With Erin."

"I know."

"And I mean," he shrugged and arched his eyebrows. "Mom and Dad aren't the greatest with advice or with examples. And…"

"Neither am I, Dric, and you know it," she said with a grin. "But I love you. And I want you to be happy, so whatever you're thinking about with Erin, I'm behind you. Every step."

"I want to ask her to move in."

"Okay." Journey nodded.

"My place is a dump."

Journey looked around the galley kitchen with a wince. Kendric's apartment wasn't a dump, but it was cramped and old. She had seen Erin's place and had to admit it had more appeal. But she had a roommate, so Kendric moving in with her was out of the question.

"Have you guys talked about it at all?"

"Just pie in the sky wedding talk."

"Really?" She blinked at him, surprised that the word had come out of his mouth.

"Not in any real way."

"Dric, you're an adult," she reminded him. "And you have a great job. You're in love with her. Talk about it. Maybe instead of moving her in here, you guys could find a place together."

Kendric regarded her silently for a long moment.

"What?" she mumbled, finally uncomfortable under his intense stare.

"I thought you would tell me it was a bad idea."

His words stung the same way it stung yesterday when Dalton had suggested the same thing.

"Why would I do that?"

"I never thought you believed in love."

Journey sighed. She cleared her throat, put her cup down, and closed the distance between them. Kendric put his arms around her when she hugged him, but she stepped away quickly.

"No." She shook her head. "I just never thought anyone could love me."

"Why would you say that?"

"If your own mother can't love you, it's hard to imagine anyone else loving you."

"Mom loves you—"

"I gotta go," she said quietly. "I don't wanna spoil my day talking about Lenore. Not when it started out so happy."

"He spent the night, didn't he?"

"He did." She nodded.

Kendric followed her to the door where she hesitated and looked back at him.

"He's working," she told him. "Something about meeting with a resident's family. But please call him later."

"Still kind of weird."

"I like the way he kisses."

"Not helping." Kendric shook his head and squeezed his eyes closed.

Journey pulled the door open and tugged her coat closer around her. "Dric."

"Hmm?"

"Do you want a baby with Erin?"

She stepped out on the porch and looked back at him.

"Maybe someday."

"Gonna get married first?"

She held her breath waiting for his answer. People didn't necessarily get married anymore because they were having a baby together. It shouldn't bother her. It wasn't even like Lenore would have loved her more or treated her better if she and Journey's father had been married when she was born. But somehow, Journey always tied the two things together in her heart.

"I'd love to marry her, Journey." Dric nodded. "What about you?"

She shook her head and stepped backwards off the

porch. "I don't know. This is all new to me. I'm gonna take it one day at a time."

She turned and hurried down the walk to her car parked at the curb.

"Journey?" Kendric called.

At the driver's door, she stopped and looked up at him. "What?"

"Are you bringing Dalton home for Christmas?"

"Yes."

Kendric's grin drew a sigh of relief from deep in her belly.

"No making out in Mom and Dad's house. I can't be traumatized like that again. Got it?"

"Kinda sounds like a dare, Dric," she called as she pulled her door open and sank into the driver's seat.

14

Journey hadn't felt this anxious for Christmas since she was a little girl. It surprised her sometimes to remember that she had started life pretty much the same as her friends, thinking her parents were like other parents and her household was the same as other households. She loved her mom with all her heart, stubbornly refusing to understand that she would never be her mother's first choice. Well, eventually, she got the message loud and clear. But for the first ten years of her life, Journey was the same as other girls her age.

When she was eleven, she watched her mom with her little brother and noticed the tenderness in her touch. Heard the gentle tone in her voice when she talked to Kendric. Lenore rarely gave Journey more than a glance—even then, and when she did, it was usually to notice something wrong and criticize her for it. When she was a preteen, her mother often scolded her for being too loud, too hyper. When she was a teenager, Lenore called her wild and trashy, never mind that Lenore usually spoke to

Journey through a cloud of smoke, with the haze of booze in her eyes. Journey learned to escape the house as often as possible, and yes, she had handed her virginity over to a boy pushing twenty when she was only fourteen. Vanessa had talked her through that night and several others, and with each year that passed, Journey grew further and further away from Lenore.

Now, as an adult, she tried to ignore her mother's criticisms. If Lenore deigned to look at her now, it was to criticize her hairstyle or her lipstick. She still referred to Journey as wild and trashy, always oozing disapproval at Journey's disdain for relationships. Thankfully, her father and Kendric made family gatherings bearable, although there were still times she wanted nothing more than to skip them.

This year would be different, Journey realized. She watched Vanessa toting Parker's three-year-old nephew around, Parker fretting over Vanessa's every move, and considered her mother's dining room table set for six this year, rather than five. It wasn't so much that she expected Lenore to treat her differently since she was bringing a guest. Journey might still crave her mother's love, Lenore's approval, but she had realized when she graduated with honors from college and Lenore nitpicked the strappy sandals she wore and called them slutty and then gone on to complain about how generic a degree in business was, Lenore would never approve of anything she did.

Nope, it wasn't that Journey thought being with Dalton would finally gain her mother's respect. It was simply that being with Dalton was more than enough; knowing that Dalton was there with her, that he would be taking her home and holding her through the night meant everything to her.

"What're you thinking about?"

Journey turned her head now to find Vanessa studying her. Her friend was no longer holding Eli. Journey swung her gaze around Nick Moore's living room to find Eli climbing on Parker by the Christmas tree. Dalton and Nick sat on opposite ends of the couch talking about health insurance. Journey's heart swelled painfully when she saw Nick's daughter Maisy inching her way closer to Dalton.

Vanessa had introduced her to Mercedes and Nick a while back, before she and Parker were expecting. Back before they were even in a relationship. Journey had been a bit skeptical about that whole deal—hooking up as a business deal to make a baby, not the fact that they had fallen in love—so she had been a little suspicious of Mercedes in the beginning. Luckily, Vanessa continued to invite her and Mercedes to do things together often enough that Journey had gotten to know both Cedes and Nick. She enjoyed spending time with them now.

And Nick's kids.

Dammit all, she wasn't sure she could do pregnancy. Motherhood. She hadn't had a mother, a good mother, so what the hell did she know about being a mom? Sure, Lenore had fed her and clothed her, but her mothering Journey had left a huge hole inside her that Journey hadn't even been able to identify until she was well into her twenties.

But she loved Maisy and Eli.

And now Vanessa was pregnant. Mercedes' friends were expecting a baby. Even Kendric was making comments about moving in with Erin and starting a family. Journey glanced at Dalton again. She wasn't ready. She loved where she was with him right at this moment in time; she needed to just hold on to that for now.

But if her friends were in a new phase of life, would she be left behind?

"Mrs. Moany invited Santa to our school."

To Journey's delight, Dalton turned a giant, sloppy grin to Maisy as she finally closed the distance between them on the couch. She didn't climb into his lap, but she simply propped her elbows on his thigh and leaned into him.

"Mrs. Mahoney," Nick corrected Maisy.

"That's what I said," Maisy groaned, sounding bored, as if she had explained herself a hundred times.

"Did you get to sit on Santa's lap?" Dalton asked her.

"I'm scared," Journey whispered. She dragged her eyes away from Dalton and looked at Vanessa again.

"Dinner's ready!" Mercedes called from the kitchen. Journey and Vanessa watched everyone climb to their feet and head to the kitchen to fill their plates. According to Vanessa, the holiday dinner just two nights before Christmas Eve had been Mercedes' idea. Even though the woman was getting married the weekend after Christmas and had to have a million things on her plate. Journey had been a dinner guest here before, so she knew from experience that Cedes could cook. Tonight, the lasagna smelled incredible, and her stomach rumbled with hunger.

"What're you afraid of?" Vanessa asked when they were alone.

"She's fixing dinner for a house full of people a few days

before Christmas, a week before her wedding. She's raising someone else's children as her own. And she wants babies." Journey took a step toward the beautiful Christmas tree in the far corner of the room. Vanessa followed her without a word. "Tab and Andrea were brave enough to fall in love and get married, and now they're having a baby. Kendric and Erin are looking at houses, and you're having Parker's baby."

Vanessa waited for her to go on.

"Someone plays this gorgeous piano." Journey swung her hand out to indicate the piano, suddenly over-whelmed by her own shortcomings.

"Actually, I think Kiara got it so Maisy and Eli would learn to play," Vanessa said softly. She tipped her head to meet Journey's eyes. "No one actually plays it. Journey? What's going on?"

Journey took a deep breath and shrugged.

"I feel so incredibly inadequate around all of you," she whispered. "I'm afraid I'll lose him."

"What?"

"I don't know how to do the things you're doing. I don't know how to be a girlfriend. A wife. I sure as hell don't know how to be a mother." She cleared her throat. "I don't even know if I want to be a mom. What if he thinks that's horrible? What if he wants kids? What if he thinks I hate kids, when really I just don't know how to deal with them?"

"Journey, sweetie—"

"Van, I can't do this. I'm crazy about him, and I keep worrying he's gonna really see me, he's gonna figure out that I'm a fake. That I can't give him what he wants, what he needs."

"Really? Because I think he just wants and needs you. The rest is extra."

"The rest isn't extra!" Journey yelped. "It's life. You guys are living. All of you guys are doing things right, and I'm still here, still stuck with this fear that I'm not doing it right."

"You're living, too, Journey," Vanessa insisted. "You're doing it right. And no matter if you stay with Dalton forever, if you get married, if you don't, if things don't work out—whatever—you're part of my life. And you'll be in my baby's life. That's not gonna change."

Journey swallowed hard and licked her lips. "What if we decide we do wanna have a baby, and it's too late? I'm not getting any younger."

"Journey."

She jumped when she heard Dalton's voice behind her. With a quick, guilty peek at Vanessa, Journey turned as Dalton approached.

"Hmm?"

"Come sit with me. I got your plate."

From the corner of her eye, Journey saw Vanessa wag her eyebrows before she slipped away.

"There's a very pretty girl flirting with me," Dalton continued. Journey laughed softly, but she didn't move to follow him.

"She's a pretty smart girl flirting with you, Dalton McKenzie."

"What's wrong?" Dalton stepped closer to her and slipped his arms around her.

"Scared," she admitted. "As much as I want to be with you, I don't know if I can do this. Be that woman."

"What woman?" He gathered her closer and held her tight.

"A wife. A mom. I'm scared to close my eyes at night because I still feel like we're a dream. How could I possibly raise a child to be strong and brave?"

"What if the only woman I want you to be is yourself?"

"And then you go and say sweet things like that." She laughed softly and swiped at her eyes. "Dammit, Dalton."

"There's no rush, Journey." He kissed the top of her head. "I'm not racing to a finish line with you. I'm enjoying the road."

She snorted and shook her head. Dalton was referring to Lenore's reason for naming her Journey.

"Life's all about the journey," she mumbled.

"All about my Journey," he agreed.

"You told me you want a family," she reminded him. "Before we were together. On the drive to the bed and breakfast, you said you wanted a family."

"I might like to have a family one day," he told her. "But right now, I want you. I don't want anything without you."

Journey pressed up on her tiptoes to meet him for a soft, sweet kiss. Mindful of the full house, she smoothed her hands up over his arms and held on.

Thank you for reading Holdin' On. If you enjoyed Journey and Dalton's story, please consider leaving a review on your favorite book site!

SNEAK PEEK OF LOVE, NASHVILLE

Chapter 1

The heavy oak door whooshed closed in slow motion behind Leah Hague. She stood for a moment just inside the bar to let her eyes adjust to the atmospheric lighting. She had expected a dingy hole in the wall honky tonk, but the interior of Left Fork was cozy and just trendy enough to make her hesitate. She wasn't here on business, unless you counted personal business, and her personal business at the moment required something dark and smoky and clientele too drunk to notice she was there to wallow. She wanted to be alone in a crowd, and she wanted cheap whiskey to burn her throat as she nursed the heartache for one more night.

She had *cried* this weekend.

Left Fork was a little too much like Mississippi Queen. She couldn't lose herself here; she couldn't forget anything here if she felt too much at home. Her eyes did another sweep of the bar, decided it wasn't as big as the

Queen, and then startled when she saw the inevitable stage at the back of the long, narrow building. She supposed every bar in Nashville had a stage and a star, or a wannabe at the very least, but until this moment, she hadn't paid a bit of attention to the music.

The guy on the stage was singing something about blame, but Leah dismissed him without so much as a second thought. She hadn't ever set foot in a bar in Nashville; she'd never been to Nashville before tonight, but she knew she was in the heart of music city. She just didn't give a damn about the music or the dreams nursed or crushed here in music city.

One more night of oblivion.

She had told herself this morning when she'd hit I-65 and headed north from Destin that she would drive half way home, soak up one more night of whatever it took to forget what she needed to forget, and go on home. Mind on Kenzi and Joe as she drove, she had to blink back tears a few times early in the drive, but her eyes had been dry by the time she crossed the Alabama state line. She wasn't a woman to cry often, and she was sick of herself a half-hour down 65.

The guy on the stage—looked the same as any other country musician to Leah—finished a song to some paltry applause. Leah raised her eyebrows and kind of hoped that the lack of noise and excitement was due to the small crowd and not a lack of enthusiasm. Then again, she didn't care. She wasn't here to commiserate with some cowboy artist or anyone, for that matter. She wasn't here to make friends.

The whole trip had been an exorcism of sorts.

A failed exorcism, but then as much as she needed to

drive the grief out, she didn't want to forget Kenzi and Joe.

"Dammit Leah." She sighed and finally took a step into the tavern. A few people glanced at her as she made her way to the bar on her strappy navy heels. Her long legs ate up the distance quickly. She set her small navy bag down as she slid onto the stool at the end of the beautiful polished wooden bar.

She smoothed the fingers of her right hand over the shiny surface with a small hum of appreciation. They paid a pretty penny for the bar at the Queen, but she had to admit it was the main focus of their business, and as such, needed to be appealing. Like this one was. Maybe she should find something else. Surely, if she looked she could find a gritty, dirty tavern where she might feel less at home and more comfortable to drown her sorrows.

The ones that would still be there in an hour or two when she slid off the barstool and made her way back into the early summer evening.

"What can I getcha?"

Leah lifted her eyes at the smoker's voice, surprised to find herself looking at a woman. Craggy-looking with severe crow's feet etched around her eyes and bushy graying brows, but definitely a woman. Her ample breasts tested the denim material that covered them, but not in a sexy way.

"Pearl."

"Excuse me?"

"Name's Pearl," the woman told her.

Leah nodded. She thought of Duncan, imagined what it would be like to walk into the Queen for the first time, belly up to the bar, and order a drink from Duncan. Hard to imagine, considering she'd known him forever. He was better-looking than Pearl, certainly, though not in any conventional way. Would he be friendly? she wondered. Well, of course he would be friendly. He was a bartender, after all. And a good guy. But would he introduce himself? Or was that a southern thing?

"I would hate to see you faced with a real tough decision," the woman muttered. Leah directed an embarrassed smirk at her, relieved to see the ghost of a smile on the woman's face.

"Jack and Coke." Leah curled her fingers into a fist and stared at the woman, inviting her to comment on her choice. Leah Hague was a wine drinker, head to toe, inside out and upside down. But she'd consumed enough Jack and Coke this weekend that she thought she might bleed amber rather than red.

The woman nodded. "Fair enough."

Leah watched her short fingers, crooked with arthritis, grab a whiskey tumbler and fill it, first with two cubes of ice, a stingy shot of Jack, and then the Coke. The woman snatched a small straw and stuck it in the glass as she set the drink in front of Leah.

"Where ya from?"

Leah took a deep breath and picked the drink up to sip it. She wasn't up for talking, but she didn't want to be rude, either. Catch 22. Her parents had raised her and her sister to be courteous, hard to shrug off that upbringing even when she was so full of bitter heartache.

"Illinois," she answered simply. Pearl nodded as if Illinois was the most interesting place in North America and then she folded her arms over her breasts and cleared her throat.

"Holler if you need something."

Leah nodded as Pearl wandered down the length of the bar. She wondered about back pain with breasts so big, even wondered why the woman hadn't had a reduction, and then she gave herself a mental shake. She set her drink down and rested her elbows on the bar.

The evening sun had been warm as she had walked the sidewalks and ducked into Left Fork. Now she shivered, thankful she had a lightweight blazer on over her cami and a bra with cups thick enough to hide her nipples, now stiff with the manufactured cold air.

The singer closed another song, and Leah was distantly aware of that same smattering of applause. But her mind was already gone, and her heart hurt again. She should call Joe. She hadn't talked to him in over a week, and she knew he would want to hear from her.

But she couldn't.

Maybe tomorrow. Maybe back at the Queen. Back to real life.

The guy started singing again, and even though Leah was not a country music fan, she recognized the song. Who didn't know the classic Conway Twitty song 'Hello, Darlin'?'" She ducked her head and rubbed her fingertips over the bridge of her nose. A headache was pushing its way between her eyes, and the whiskey was a bad idea.

She picked the drink up and sipped again. She didn't love the taste of it. Duncan handled the hard liquor purchases. Now and then he involved the rest of them in a tasting, but Leah had never acquired the *taste* for it. Just the need to be numb.

Unfortunately, she had to drive tonight. She had picked her hotel for that reason. Far enough away from downtown that she couldn't walk, therefore she couldn't stagger out of here, bombed on her ass.

"Kitchen's open until nine," Pearl told her as she made her way back down the bar. Leah started to thank her, to let her know she wouldn't be ordering, but Pearl only slid a menu toward her across the bar and moseyed on to lean into a conversation several stools down.

The kids would be out of school now. Leah huffed out a harsh breath and tucked her hair behind her ears. Would that make it easier for Joe? Someone around to talk to? Leah bit her lip and squeezed her eyes closed. Wasn't that part of the reason he'd packed up their lives and moved them all the way across the country?

But wouldn't it be harder, too? Adelynn and Liam were busy kids; neither drove yet, and they both played summer sports, and Joe was working now. Running Edison to daycare.

Edison.

Leah dragged her fingers back through her thick hair and picked up the glass again. With Edison still in her heart, sipping time was gone. She gulped a healthy swallow and then sniffled when her eyes and her nose burned. She wondered what she was supposed to do if she'd already hit the spot where the whiskey wasn't working anymore.

"Hey, darlin'."

She shivered, though she wasn't exactly cold now. Even that stingy shot of Jack was enough to warm her. The deep voice that had just been singing was now so close to her ear, she felt the warmth of his breath there on her skin. Just a little bit turned on now by that delicious voice and a whole lot irritated that her body would betray her that easily, Leah ignored the tingle in her fingertips and the little hum low in her stomach.

Because she wanted to look, she refused to turn her head in his direction. Good grief. Was she hard up, so stressed that two words from some wannabe Nashville star could start her up? Instead, she picked up her drink and sipped again. Set the glass down with a steady hand, eyed the elegant white gold watch on her wrist—she'd been here all of seven minutes—and finally turned her head just a tiny bit to the left with the intention of telling Nashville she wasn't interested.

Deep, dark, emerald green eyes caught hers in what she meant to be a quick once over.

Damn. She was wrong.

This guy didn't look a thing like any other musician she had ever seen. And no, she wasn't often up close and personal with musicians of any sort. But she knew it just the same, because she'd never seen such a gorgeous man. Anywhere. Leah struggled to swallow as she tore her eyes from his intense, probing gaze. That hum in her stomach kicked up a notch as she took in the razor sharp cheekbones, the thick dark eyebrows, and the thick dark hair that fell over Nashville's forehead and curled just a bit behind his ears and over the back of his neck.

The slate blue t-shirt he wore was stretched taut over broad shoulders, and his legs appeared to go on forever. Leah tried to swallow again, but her mouth was bone dry. Being that she was five ten, she liked tall men.

Not that she was looking for any man, tall or not.

He was smiling when she dragged her eyes back up over his denim-clad legs (She wondered briefly if he was wearing Wranglers. Was that a thing? Did cowboys wear

Wrangler jeans?) and his chest (also broad, not that she was really measuring) and his face. It was the ego in the smile that brought her back to her senses and saved her.

Sex with a body like that would work a hell of a lot better than whiskey to clear her head. But she didn't have time for it. No time or desire to deal with that kind of arrogance.

Still, she couldn't deny that he was the most perfect-looking man she'd ever seen. Heart still beating at the base of her throat, she looked back at her tumbler and picked it up again. Sex with that body might work better than whiskey to clear her head, but whiskey would be the far better hangover to nurse on the remainder of her drive home tomorrow.

He watched her sip her drink. When she looked at him a second time, he toned the smile down some, and rather than ego, she noticed the scruff on his jaw and perfect white teeth, and something that looked like charm.

Really, Leah?

Maybe in the south charm was equivalent to ego.

She turned her barstool a fraction of an inch toward him and noticed with amusement when his eyes grew wider. Drink still in hand, she shook her head.

"I'm not gonna sleep with you, Nashville."

Surprised to sound in control when she was still telling herself she wasn't interested in finding out what the scruff on his face would feel like in that spot where her neck and shoulder met, she snorted softly when he sagged his shoulders in defeat and jokingly ducked his chin a bit.

"I would never assume such a thing, ma'am," he promised her.

Ma'am?

Did he really just call her ma'am?

"Right." She nodded as she raised her glass and tilted her head back. When she remembered she had finished the whiskey, she crunched a piece of ice and put the glass back on the bar.

"Can I buy you a drink?" he offered. Leah turned her barstool back square to the bar and rested her elbows on opposite sides of her drink. Yes, she needed another. No, she didn't want this guy to buy her anything. Any further involvement here would be a bad idea.

"What's your name?" He turned square on his seat and rested his arms on the bar, too. Only he laid his forearms long ways on the bar and folded one hand over the other. He looked at her, though, and Leah ignored the way his t-shirt molded those wide shoulders. Instead she focused on his face, and it hit her again. That...charm.

He appeared friendly.

Were guys this drop-dead good-looking friendly?

When she didn't answer him, he arched his eyebrows and tilted his head.

"Leah." Her voice was gruff this time, and she had a flash of memory suddenly of Kenzi and Joe. Reminded that she wasn't here to make friends, that she wasn't here to have fun, she turned away from him again and stared straight ahead. The prerequisite mirror behind the bar hung low, and Leah was taller than most women, and unfortunately, she found herself staring at a woman who looked to be a good ten years older than her thirty. Maybe Nashville thought she was a cougar.

She almost laughed at that; but when she looked his way again and found him watching her, she changed her mind. He certainly wasn't jailbait. Wasn't ready for a midlife crisis, either, but he'd most definitely grown out of that young cute guy vibe.

Not that it mattered.

"What're you drinking, Leah?"

She wiggled a bit on her barstool when she felt another shiver niggling at the base of her spine. That voice. God, she would hear that voice saying her name in her dreams for nights to come.

"Jack and Coke," she answered, because she desperately needed another right now.

"Okay." Nashville nodded. Leah saw him lift a finger, and a few moments later, Pearl was standing across from them. "Pearl, Leah would like another Jack and Coke."

To her credit, the woman did look at Leah as she went through the same motions to make her another drink, as if checking to make sure she did want another.

"Getcha anything off the menu, hon?"

Leah's shoulders stiffened. She hated to be called hon. Hated when strangers did it, even if they thought they were being friendly. If she heard Duncan say something like that at the Queen, she'd sock him in the gut or stomp on his toes.

"No, thank you." She flashed Pearl a small, tight smile.

"You hungry, Trace?" The woman turned to Nashville, and her face completely rearranged itself into something sweet and almost pretty. Leah flicked her eyes from Pearl to Nashville and back to Pearl. Okay, so Nashville wasn't a kid, but Pearl looked old enough to be his grandmother.

Nashville grinned sheepishly and ducked his head.

"I'm always hungry, Pearl. You know that."

"Don't I know it?" Pearl agreed. "I'll have 'em start you a—"

The woman stopped talking when Nashville shook his head.

"No time," he told her. Pearl shot a quick glance at the stage and then looked back at him.

"Suit yourself."

He smiled as Pearl made her way back down the bar.

"Leah what?"

Leah laughed softly, but she only bit her lip and shook her head.

"Where are you from?"

Hoping that his comment to Pearl about no time meant that he had to get back to the stage any minute, Leah turned on the stool to face him.

"Why does it matter?"

Nashville hesitated, but he eventually turned sideways again to face her, and Leah's eyes were drawn down over his lean-looking torso and his long legs. When she looked at his face again, he shrugged and offered her a small smile.

"Guess it doesn't," he said quietly. "You're passing through?"

"Yes." She nodded. "Back on the road tomorrow."

The wince was almost unnoticeable, but disappointment settled over his face like a mask.

"Okay." He took a deep breath and stood, giving Leah a full view of his long, broad frame. "Well...I guess I can say I had the pleasure of buying the most beautiful woman in the world a drink in a Nashville bar called Left Fork."

Leah blinked at him, stunned by his words and even more so by his soft, sincere tone. Sure, he probably said that to every woman he bumped into in Left Fork and every other damned bar in Tennessee. But it took a certain kind of man to sound sincere, and that look in his eyes zapped her. Not in her belly. Not in any special spots. Right smack in the heart.

The one that had already broken over Kenzi and Joe and the kids.

Leah opened her mouth to say something—anything—but Nashville smiled again. Frozen in place, she watched him reach toward her, and when she realized he was going to touch her, she held her breath. Her heart thundered now in her chest, Kenzi and Joe be damned, and her eyelids fluttered closed as he brushed her hair off her shoulder.

"Safe travels, Leah."

The tenderness in his voice stroked her skin as she had assumed he was going to do with his fingers. Goose-bumps broke out on her flesh, but when she opened her eyes again, Nashville was gone.

Her breath came back in a rush, and her cheeks flushed with warmth that had nothing at all to do with the whiskey in the glass she still held. Realizing her hand shook just a bit, she turned back to the bar and put the drink down.

"Trace has that effect on a lot of women," Pearl told her. Leah huffed out another hard breath and nodded, chin tucked to her chest.

Maybe she should have taken him up on his offer. If he had her this worked up just from brushing her hair off her shoulder, she wondered what he could do for her alone in a bed.

…Trace has that effect on a lot of women…

Pearl's words came back to her. Hammered her right between the eyes.

Of course he had that effect on a lot of women. She lifted her chin when he strummed his acoustic guitar again. She refused to look that way, but from the intimate sound of his voice, she wondered if he was leaning in closer to the microphone.

His voice, a bit softer now, sang about a woman and her beautiful body.

"Haven't seen one get to him like you, though."

Leah blinked at Pearl. She most certainly wasn't here to listen to the chronicles of Nashville's pickups.

If Kenzi were here right now, she would give Leah an earful about not climbing the barstool and riding the singing cowboy bareback.

"He never comes to the bar until his last set's over," Pearl announced. "And everyone's gone."

To read more about Leah and Nashville, go to:

books2read.com/lovenashville

ABOUT THE AUTHOR

Tracy Broemmer is the author of several contemporary romance novels including The Mississippi Queen Trilogy, the H Books, and Wedding Day Shenanigans. Tracy also writes women's fiction and is the author of the Williams Legacy series as well as several stand-alone titles.

Tracy's books have been called gripping, emotional, and timely, and readers describe her characters as real and relatable.

Tracy lives in Midwestern Illinois with her husband of 29 years.

Find more about Tracy's books here: www. broemmerbooks.com

ALSO BY TRACY BROEMMER

Women's Fiction Novels:

Luther's Cross (Writing as Therese Kinkaide)

Luther's Cross 10th Anniversary Edition (Tracy Broemmer)

Fairytale (Writing as Therese Kinkaide)

Just Like Them (Writing as Therese Kinkaide)

Small Hours (Writing as Therese Kinkaide)

Picket Fences

Two Story Home

Green-Eyed Girl

Say Everything

Come Home For Christmas

Sketching Litchfield Lake

Ever, Again

Safe as Houses

Damsel

Every Little Thing, Lorelei Bluffs, Book 1

Two A.M., Lorelei Bluffs, Book 2

Blind, Lorelei Bluffs, Book 3

Leaving July, Lorelei Bluffs, Book 4

Hesitation Marks, Lorelei Bluffs, Book 5

Four Letter Words, Lorelei Bluffs, Book 6

See Kate, Lorelei Bluffs, Book 7

Contemporary Romance Short Stories:

Perfect Pictures, The Wine Tasting Series, Traminette

Coming Home, The Wine Tasting Series, Edelweiss

Save Me Every Dance, The Wine Tasting Series, Rosé

Marry Me, The Wine Tasting Series, Shiraz

Birthday Wishes, The Wine Tasting Series, Muscat

Dad Jeans, The Wine Tasting Series, Vignoles